Dedication

This book is dedicated to all of the girls in the A Life of Faith Girls Club. May you always remember this powerful promise from your Heavenly Father:

For I am the Lord, your God,
who takes hold of your right hand
and says to you, Do not fear; I will help you.
—Isaiah 41:13

— Table of Contents —

— Table of Contents —

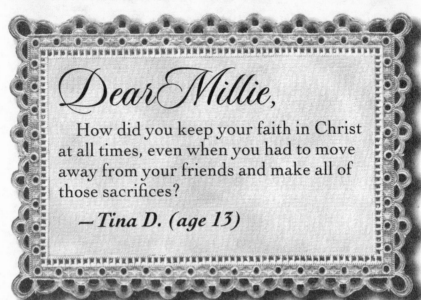

Dear Millie,

How did you keep your faith in Christ at all times, even when you had to move away from your friends and make all of those sacrifices?

— *Tina D. (age 13)*

Dear Tina,

If you want a faith that is unwavering, you must have a personal love relationship with Jesus. You can't hold true to Him to the point of sacrifice if you don't really know and love Him. This is certainly a learning process.

With each challenge that I encountered during my move and the rebuilding of our lives in Indiana, I constantly turned to my relationship with God for help and support. In turn, God showed Himself faithful to me, and that strengthened my own faith in Him. As I trusted Jesus with each situation, the roots of my faith grew deeper and stronger, as did my love for Him.

Staying Rooted in the Lord

"So then, just as you received Christ Jesus as Lord, continue to live in him, ROOTED and built up in him, strengthened in the faith as you were taught, and overflowing with thankfulness" (Colossians 2:6–7).

"And I pray that you, being ROOTED and established in love, may have power, together with all the saints, to grasp how wide and long and high and deep is the love of Christ, and to know this love that surpasses knowledge— that you may be filled to the measure of all the fullness of God" (Ephesians 3:17–19).

God will sustain you with His perfect love.

Don't worry about how you may hold up in trials. Just seek to love God each day. When the storms come, turn to Him, just like I did. God will sustain you with His perfect love, and you will find that your own life of faith is strengthened and deeply rooted in Him.

Love, Millie

Dear Millie,

I want so badly to read the Bible and find out the answers to my questions, but I don't know where to find them! I want to act, dress, talk, and be as Jesus, but where do I find these answers in the Bible?

— Jessica F. (age 13)

Dear Jessica,

I am so blessed by your burning desire to search God's Word and learn how to live for Him! One way to understand how to live for God is to study the life of Jesus, because we are to "imitate" His life (His attitude, behavior, etc.).

I encourage you to start reading one of the four Gospels, like the book of John, found in the New Testament. Read it to get to know the personality of Jesus, and ask God to open your mind to the understanding of the Scriptures.

8

Another good book to read is the book of James, also in the New Testament. It has great instruction for living a life honoring to God. There are also many wonderful study guides at your local Christian bookstore. We have one called *Millie's Life Lessons: Adventures in Trusting God.*

As you begin to dive into the Word, pray for understanding and press into your relationship with God. You will be rewarded. God will draw near to you and begin to answer the questions in your heart.

Study the life of Jesus, because we are to "imitate" His life.

Love, Millie

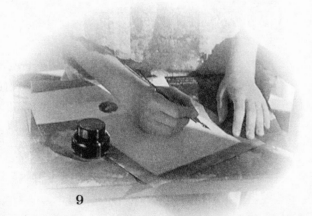

Dear Millie,

I recently gave my life to Christ (I have been a Christian for ten years and I wanted to serve God with my life, not just my heart) and ever since then I have been going through a lot of testing and God has been working on my spirit. I want to grow in my relationship and I was wondering what I could do to become more like Him in ways such as prayer, faith, and humility. I appreciate your help.

—Katie P. (age 13)

Dear Katie,

Your sincere, wholehearted devotion to Jesus really thrills me! I know that God has prepared you for something special. Trust Him to work in your life through His Holy Spirit. He will see to it that you are equipped for the plans He has for you. Your responsibility now and always is to seek after Him with all your heart and be faithful to the foundational practices necessary for spiritual growth: Bible study, prayer, praise, fellowship, and witnessing. All these are very important to stay strong in the Lord.

The testing you are going through does not surprise me. You have already understood that this is how the Lord forms His character into us. Do not despise the trials. Press into them, rejoice in them, and let them be your tutors. Resistance in our lives serves to make us stronger. Let God's Word comfort you during these times of testing. Look at 1 Peter 4:12–19.

> *As you seek Him, He will teach you and guide you in His ways.*

I guess if I could give you a few nuggets they would be—pursue love and humility; hate what is evil, but cling to what is good (see Romans 12:9); and seek to really know God as a *person*, trusting Him with all your heart. As you seek Him, He will teach you and guide you in His ways. Read Isaiah 50:4–5.

I want to really encourage you, Katie. You can have as much of God as you want. Nothing can hold you back from fulfilling the plans God has for you. Go for it! Your life will be full of rewards, blessings, and adventures.

Love, Millie

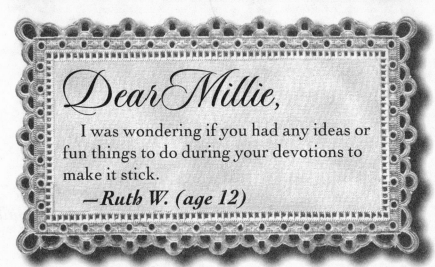

Dear Millie,

I was wondering if you had any ideas or fun things to do during your devotions to make it stick.

—*Ruth W. (age 12)*

Dear Ruth,

I'm so glad you asked this question because it shows you really want God's Word to change you. We don't read the Bible to get information—we read the Bible to get a transformation. There is a big difference in the two. You cannot read the Bible like a novel. You must realize that God's Word has a lot of power in it. It is like a stick of dynamite. When you read something in the Scripture and then believe it and obey, you have applied a lighted match to that stick of dynamite. It's no longer information stored in your head; it now touches and changes your heart.

I would recommend using a journal when you are reading the Bible. Try using colored gel pens so it's more fun when you are writing. Use your journal to record what Scriptures you read and what God speaks to you

personally. We have a beautiful faith journal that will
make your devotional time practical, ordered, and fun. It
is called *Millie's Daily Diary*. You might want to check it
out.

If you don't mind marking in your Bible, use colored
highlighters to mark passages that are special to you as
you read. You can even make
notations in the margins of your
Bible. Look for key words that
are repeated and mark them. You
can write the date next to a
Scripture that you feel is a special
promise to you.

*I hope some of these
ideas help to enrich your
devotional time.*

If you don't like marking in your Bible, try using
brightly colored sticky-notes. They come in all sizes.
You can stick the tiny notes in your Bible to mark
pages or passages that you really feel are important to
review. Copy verses on the larger sizes and then stick
them to your mirror, refrigerator, etc., so that throughout the day you can be reminded of them.

I hope some of these ideas help to enrich your devotional time and serve to keep you hungering to be
transformed by God's Word.

Love, Millie

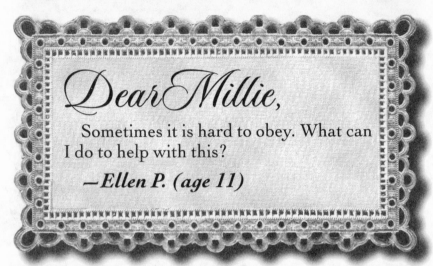

Dear Millie,

Sometimes it is hard to obey. What can I do to help with this?

—Ellen P. (age 11)

Dear Ellen,

Obedience is hard for all of us because it forces us to deny our own self-will. If we are to obey, we have to put someone else's will above our own. 1 John 5:3 says, "This is love for God: to obey his commands. And his commands are not burdensome."

We see in this verse a relationship between love and obedience. If you really love someone, you want to please him or her. Continue your quest to know and love God. The more you understand how great His love is for you, the more you will want to please Him in return.

Obedience puts you in the position to receive protection, safety, and blessing. Your parents give you certain guidelines to obey because they know it is for your well-being. This is all the more true with your Heavenly Father. You also know that if you choose to disobey, you will fall into some form of danger or harm.

Obedience puts you in the position to receive protection, safety, and blessing.

If you understand how important obedience is and how pleasing it is to God that you obey, this will possibly motivate you to work harder at it. It still comes down to you making the choice to obey. You must want to do what is right. Ask God to help you, and faithfully confess your sins to Him and others when you fail.

May God release much grace for you in this area.

Love, Millie

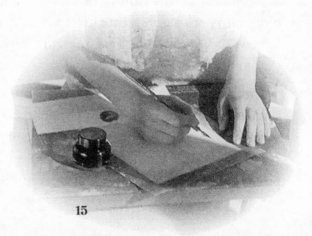

Dear Millie,

I've just decided to become a Christian and I found out that it isn't easy. So whenever I do something, I think of what you would do and it sort of helps. Is there any other way to become a true Christian like you?

—*Ashley C. (age 10)*

Dear Ashley,

Welcome to the family of God! I'm so glad that you have chosen to give your life to Jesus at such a young age. What incredible blessings are now yours because you are a child of God!

I am honored that you consider me a role model and try to live as I do. Jesus is the ultimate role model and you can read all about Him in the Gospels (Matthew, Mark, Luke, and John, found in the New Testament part of your Bible). The best thing you can do to really grow into a true Christian is to read your Bible and obey the truths you find there. I was raised on God's Word. It became the anchor that held me through all my trials and sorrows.

You are right in observing that the life of a Christian is not easy. Jesus never promised it would be easy, but He promised that in everything He would lead us in victory (Romans 8:37) and that His presence would always be with us (Romans 8:38–39). He promised us perfect peace, joy, and love that can never be taken away from us (John 16:33, 14:27). Keep reading His Word and you will find many more wonderful promises for you!

Jesus never promised it would be easy, but He promised that in everything He would lead us in victory.

Love, Millie

Dear Millie,

I have a problem. I have grown up in a loving, Christian home all my life, but my best friend has been a bad influence on my life over the past year. I started listening to secular music, swearing, talking on Instant Messenger, going in bad chat rooms, etc. The thing is; my parents don't know. I feel so guilty! My life is all confused right now. In my heart I want to be the Christian my parents want me to be, but another part of me is saying, "No! I want to do what I want to do." I feel like a big fake, pretending to be this perfect little Christian, but inside I'm really dying. I know I am pretty selfish and I am afraid of God. I don't feel like I can pray to Him anymore, and I don't feel His protection over me, which is scary. I feel lost, alone, and insecure. Please help me.

—Really Lost in Life (age 13)

Dear Really Lost in Life,

My sweet, precious lamb! Thank you for writing and sharing your struggle with me. There is hope for you to turn this situation around and become the woman of God you are truly meant to be. You will soar with joy, peace, and a strong sense of destiny when you turn your heart back to the Lord.

When sin begins to rule our actions, we feel separated from God, confused, frustrated, and frightened, just as you are feeling now.

It is easy to get back on track, but you have to *want* to. I know you desire change, but you must make some tough decisions in order to move forward. It starts with having a talk with the friend who is badly influencing your behavior. Lovingly explain to her that you want to live for God and that your current actions are dragging you down and filling you with anxiety and fear. Maybe she is experiencing the same inner turmoil and you could be the one to influence her toward godliness. In the end you may not be as close anymore, but there are always sacrifices that we must make if we are going to follow wholeheartedly after Jesus.

Next, be honest with your parents. They will help get you back on track. Finally, re-commit your heart back to Jesus, and spend some time in prayer and repentance for your behavior. God will bring cleansing and healing to your soul when you confess your sins.

Do not delay. The longer you resist, the more difficult it is to turn and change your current behavior. And always remember, when God forgives, He forgets, and you have a clean slate.

Love, Millie

Dear Millie,

I have a lot of friends whom I really like, but many of them believe in talking in tongues and visions and things I don't agree with! What am I supposed to say to them? I try to answer the way God wants me to but I don't know what that is. Please tell me how to respond.

—*Kimberly A. (age 13)*

Dear Kimberly,

It is great hearing from you and I appreciate your question.

First, it's important to remember that the Scriptures are our ultimate authority in these matters (2 Timothy 3:16-17). Each Christian must seek out the answers by studying the Bible to see what God has to say. However, good Christian people will sometimes differ in their honest interpretation of the Scriptures. If we allow differing opinions to cause divisions and arguments among us, then we lose sight of the Spirit of

Christ, which leads us in love and unity. "Everyone should be quick to listen, slow to speak and slow to become angry" (James 1:19). Listen carefully to one another. Be humble, teachable, study the Bible carefully, and ask the Lord to lead you into all truth. And above

> *Seek to show love to your friends — no matter what your differences.*

all, seek to show love to your friends — no matter what your differences. "And over all these virtues put on love, which binds them all together in perfect unity" (Colossians 3:14).

Love, Millie

Dear Millie,

I have a problem. My friend (who is not a Christian) and I got into a fight about religion. I asked her if I could show her some verses because she had started reading the Bible. But then she said she didn't want to listen anymore and we got into an argument. What should I do? We haven't talked in 3 months. I sent her a letter, telling her what I thought and apologizing. But she said the letter made her madder. Should we end this friendship? We always get into fights and she is not exactly the greatest friend. But part of me wants to stay friends to witness to her. But the way things are going, I'll never be able to do that. What should I do?

—*Madelyn B. (age 12)*

Dear Madelyn,

I really appreciate your desire to witness to this friend. I know you really care for her, and I think that is what will speak to her more than any words right now. It sounds like she is tired of being preached at. You can never argue anyone into the Kingdom of God, but you can demonstrate the Kingdom of God through love.

> *You can never argue anyone into the Kingdom of God.*

Love will draw them, and that's what it's all about anyway—God's love, not what we should or shouldn't do, or who's right and who's wrong. She needs to know that God loves her. Let her feel God's love, mercy, and grace through you. Back off from any kind of "instruction" and just simply enjoy being her friend. If she will spend time with you, do things you enjoy together. Listen to her (without giving your opinion). Give her room to talk and share her feelings and opinions. Make her feel accepted. She already knows where you stand. In time, she may feel secure enough in your friendship to ask questions or to hear your heart, but that must be earned.

"Be devoted to one another in brotherly love. Honor one another above yourselves" (Romans 12:10).

Thanks for desiring to be a friend who will love as Jesus loves.

Love, Millie

Dear Millie,

I have a question. I'm sort of weird...
not bad weird, and in a way I'm proud of
being so different! The thing is, when
you're obsessed with words like spiffy
and yoodles, and even gas prices, it's not
easy to make friends. I go to a Christian
school and nobody makes fun of me, but
I can't say I'm the most popular person
to be around, you know? Any insight or
advice would be helpful! Thanks!

—Lauren H. (age 12)

Dear Lauren,

I know how you feel. When I moved from Lansdale,
Ohio, to Pleasant Plains, Indiana, I felt very different
from everyone else. But I learned that being different
can be good, especially if you are becoming the unique
person God created you to be.

God loves variety in His creation! No two people are alike. I'm glad you are not feeling embarrassed about your uniqueness. However, I would caution you to be careful that you are not drawing your identity only on the notion that you are *different* from others. Let me explain.

Some people try to find their identify in *being like* everyone else, while others try to find their identity in *being different* from everybody else. As Christians, we don't need to base our identity around

> *Find your total purpose and fulfillment in the One who loves you perfectly!*

what people think of us. We now find that we are totally accepted and loved by God, and we can feel good about ourselves because we know how God feels about us. We become God-focused, not self- or people-focused. Then we are truly free to be who we are without needing to strive for the approval of others.

So regardless of how you compare to others, just keep striving to find your total purpose and fulfillment in the One who loves you perfectly!

"The body is a unit, though it is made up of many parts; and though all its parts are many, they form one body," says 1 Corinthians 12:12.

Enjoy your uniqueness and may your life humbly glorify the Lord.

Love, Millie

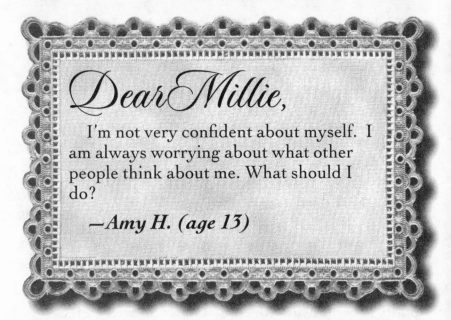

Dear Millie,

I'm not very confident about myself. I am always worrying about what other people think about me. What should I do?

—*Amy H. (age 13)*

Dear Amy,

Thanks for being so transparent! This is a battle worth fighting because trying to please people to feel good about yourself is both a trap and an impossible task.

You have been looking to people to find approval, acceptance, love, and esteem. You feel like you have to earn it, and keep earning it. It's never enough. You will keep going to the well of human affection and keep coming back thirsty. If you are looking to people to meet a need that only God can meet, then you have in some ways become a slave to people.

What really matters is what God says about you. You must get your focus totally on the Lord. Know what His Word says about how precious you are, and then begin to believe it. Let your mind be renewed by the truth in God's Word. When you believe the truth, you will then believe correctly about yourself. You will see yourself as God sees you. This will bring you to a very balanced way of thinking which Romans 12:3 calls "sober judgment." We judge ourselves or evaluate ourselves according to God's Word.

> *What really matters is what God says about you.*

Colossians 3:3–4 says that your life is hidden in Christ. Your identity IS Christ. When you really get this, you will begin to walk in boldness because of who you are in Christ. Colossians 3:12 says that you are chosen of God, holy and dearly loved. And 1 Peter 2:9–10 says that you belong to God. You are chosen, holy, and royal.

I cannot emphasize enough how important it is that you know and believe God's Word. This is what will change your incorrect thinking. Make your thoughts line up with what God says. Your attitudes, emotions, and behavior will all come into agreement with what you believe.

Lift your eyes to the Lord and place all your hope, confidence, and trust in Him.

Love, Millie

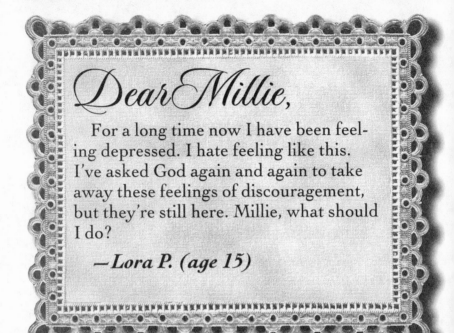

Dear Millie,

For a long time now I have been feeling depressed. I hate feeling like this. I've asked God again and again to take away these feelings of discouragement, but they're still here. Millie, what should I do?

—*Lora P. (age 15)*

Dear Lora,

Thanks for sharing so openly. It is important that you get delivered from this. God does not want you to live depressed. He sent Jesus to die for your sins and to give you peace, joy, healing, and well-being.

Somewhere, Satan is lying to you and keeping you from believing the truth in God's Word. When you believe a lie, you are submitting your emotions to the effects of the lie, which cause depression, fear, insecurity, etc. You have to search your heart and ask yourself where you do not believe that God's Word is true for you. Know what God says about you in the Bible.

I really feel like you need to get with an older woman who is a strong Christian. It could be someone in your family or someone in your church, but get with someone whom you trust and respect and be very honest about your struggles. You need someone else praying with you and helping you find out where this depression is coming from. When you find the source, then take the Word of God and His promises and begin to believe God. Use your Bible as a sword against the depression (Ephesians 6:17). Your belief in Jesus and His Word

Use your Bible as a sword against the depression.

will tear down any attack from the enemy, but you must get militant and go after this thing (2 Corinthians 10:3–5). Don't forget, we are in a battle. In 1 Peter 5:8 we are told that Satan is prowling around roaring like a lion looking for someone to devour. Verse 9 says to resist him, standing firm in your faith. You have not been destined to live in depression. God's children receive an inheritance of joy, peace, love, and a sound mind (2 Timothy 1:7). Fight for what is yours through Jesus!

Don't stop until you get totally set free from this depression. May God lead you to the right person who can help you.

Love, Millie

Dear Millie,

I have a constant problem with wanting to buy cool clothes. My parents are against certain types of jeans, shorts, spaghetti straps, etc., and I really like those. I also feel like I am a good Christian and if I'm perfect and polite then I never have any fun and no one (that is, the people I want) will like me. Please help me. I want to be "cool".

—*Leslie S. (age 14)*

Dear Leslie,

I understand your desire to be cool and fit in. The pull of this world is very strong on teens. Satan knows you are struggling with your identity and self-esteem at this age. He will try to deceive you into thinking that in order for you to feel fulfilled and accepted you must look and act a certain way.

Although there is nothing inherently wrong with wearing fashionable clothes, we must be careful that we do not become preoccupied with our appearances. Romans 12:2 says, "Do not conform any longer to the pattern of this world, but be transformed by the renewing of your mind. Then you will be able to test and approve what God's will is — his good, pleasing and perfect will." Getting too caught up in fashions or fads can distract you from what's really important in life — knowing Jesus. Find a balance and really search your heart's motives for why you want to be cool and accepted by a certain group of people. And remember, honoring your parents' wishes when it comes to your choice of clothing and friends is godly and pleasing to God the Father.

The pull of this world is very strong on teens.

You will soon find that anything the world has to offer will always leave you empty and wanting more. Only God can give us perfect satisfaction, contentment, and wholeness. Be careful that you're not looking to the world in any way for your fulfillment. I am convinced that nobody has more fun than Christians who have surrendered themselves fully to God! Life with Christ is an adventure like no other! My Aunt Wealthy is one of the strongest Christians I know, and every day of her life seems like an adventure!

I really appreciate your honesty. Thanks for writing.

Love, Millie

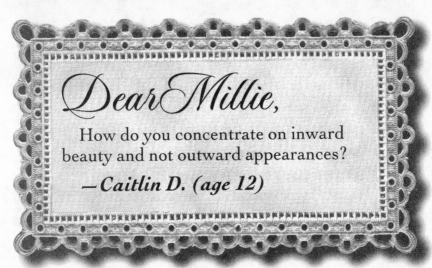

Dear Millie,

How do you concentrate on inward beauty and not outward appearances?

—*Caitlin D. (age 12)*

Dear Caitlin,

This is definitely a challenge for young girls and I appreciate that you are opening your heart to the Lord in this area.

1 Peter 3:3–6 addresses this issue of beauty for Christian women. In the eyes of God, true beauty begins within the heart—a gentle, submissive, humble spirit is beautiful. Remember that man looks on the outward appearance, whereas God looks at the heart (1 Samuel 16:7).

If you truly desire to know God's ways, you will value what He values also. You will see the spiritual as more important than the physical. Now, I don't believe in excesses. I don't believe this passage in 1 Peter is telling women that they cannot adorn themselves with makeup, jewelry, nice clothes, etc. God made us to want to look nice and enjoy these things. Just make sure you are not placing more value on the external than your internal qualities and characteristics.

Be very careful that your identity or self-esteem is not wrapped up in how you look. If you do, you will find your self-worth decreasing as your outward beauty decreases. This is why many women will pay a fortune for cosmetic surgery to keep their outward appearance beautiful. Their hope is in their looks, yet they are empty inside. This is a horrible trap that the world imposes on women. Let the Lord establish His standard of beauty for you, not Hollywood. Your outward beauty will fade, but 1 Peter 3:4 says the beauty of a pure heart will never fade.
1 Peter 1:24–25 says, "All men are like grass, and all their glory [flesh] is like the flowers of the field; the grass withers and the flowers fall, but the word of the Lord stands forever."

Let the Lord establish His standard of beauty for you, not Hollywood.

Thanks for writing, Caitlin. May you blossom into a beautiful woman of God — inside and out.

Love, Millie

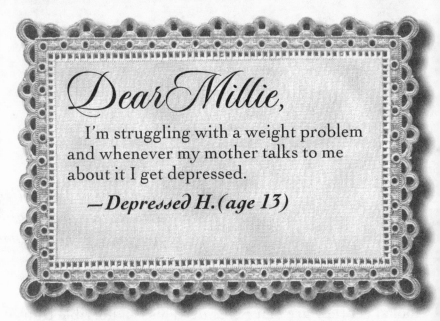

Dear Millie,

I'm struggling with a weight problem and whenever my mother talks to me about it I get depressed.

—Depressed H. (age 13)

Dear Depressed,

Well, let's tackle that depression before we tackle the weight problem. Depression comes from believing a lie. Satan makes you feel depressed. He makes you feel bad about yourself. He tells you that you cannot lose weight and he tells you other negative things. He is the father of lies. Ask yourself if there are any lies that you have believed about yourself and your weight.

Philippians 4:13 says, "I can do everything through him who gives me strength." Ask God to give you just enough strength to take the first step with your weight problem. If you look at the problem and how far you have to go, you will get depressed. The Lord gives us grace sufficient for one day at a time. For each day, follow the guidelines you and your mom decide on. If you need to start slowly, then do so. Maybe it's just avoiding certain foods. Or maybe you should start with a regular exercise that you enjoy, like biking, tennis, or swimming. When you have a good handle on that, try to add something else to your plan. You will be amazed at how much better you will feel about yourself when you get control over your weight. You will feel better physically too.

Depression comes from believing a lie.

Self-discipline is such an important character quality. As Christians, we are to be disciplined soldiers in God's army (2 Timothy 2:3–4). If we are able to discipline ourselves in physical areas, it will also help us be disciplined in spiritual areas, such as having devotions and going to church. If we train ourselves to be disciplined, we allow for only one master in our life — Jesus. We are not to be slaves to anything else such as food, television, movies, music, etc.

Keep your eyes on Jesus. He is the Bread of Life (John 6:35). Let the Bread of Life fill your soul and meet your every need. Let Him satisfy the cravings of your soul, and the cravings of your flesh will be subdued.

Remember, you can do all things through Christ.

Love, Millie

Dear Millie,

I have a baby-sitting job that is a lot of work. The four-year-old doesn't like me that much, so I try to spend more time with her, but there is also a twenty-month-old and two eight-year-old twins. It is very stressful. What should I do when I get that way? I usually take a deep breath and keep going, but I baby-sit frequently, and I get very over-whelmed. Can you help?

—*Allison J. (age 13)*

Dear Allison,

As the oldest of eight children, I have seven younger mischievous brothers and sisters, and I can really understand where you are coming from! Baby-sitting is a lot of work and responsibility, and four children are quite a bit for one as young as you.

Why don't you talk with your parents about it? It is not good for a 13-year-old to feel so stressed. If you are feeling this way, it is a warning sign that something needs to lighten up for you. You may want to reduce your days to twice a week or shorten the length of time each day. Ask God to order your steps and to show you His will.

Don't ever feel you are trapped in a situation. It is important to always keep things before the Lord and stay open to adjustments. Always work things out with your parents. Make sure you are keeping your time with the Lord each day. This will help you stay in His peace and you will be able to discern His will for you also.

If you are feeling this way, it is a warning sign that something needs to lighten up for you.

May the Lord give you His wisdom.

Love, Millie

Dear Millie,

Right now it seems like my life has been taken over with schoolwork! Speeches, projects, and other things take up so much of my time I barely get any exercise, and we never get gym class! I have different activities, like piano, that also take up a lot of my time. I do well in school, but I am always having trouble with projects. Do you have any advice to help me get more free time?

—*Christina V. (age 13)*

Dear Christina,

When my family moved to the Indiana frontier, I was very busy with many new tasks and jobs. I realized very quickly the importance of having free time. Your life needs the healthy balance of work, rest, exercise, and recreation. You will have to get very ordered and disciplined with your schedule to have this balance.

Organizing Your Time

One suggestion for better managing your time is to keep a journal for one week and record how you are spending your time each day. At the end of the week, carefully examine your record and ask yourself: Am I wasting chunks of time by watching too much TV, phone calls, chatting online, sleeping too long, etc.?

Maybe you are simply trying to do too much and need to cut out an activity until school is over. It may also help to make a schedule for your days as well as your

Time is a gift that God has given to us. We must be very wise how we use it!

weekends. If you know you have a project due, schedule in time during the week to work on it so it doesn't hit at the last minute. Get yourself one of those neat Day-timers that will help organize your days better. Your parents can help you with this. Getting organized will really help you maximize your days. You will feel a sense of confidence and accomplishment as you discipline yourself and get organized with your time. Time is a gift that God has given to us. We must be very wise how we use it!

It is good for you to develop these skills now while you are young. You will really need them when you are older. God is a God of order. Just look at nature. He will certainly help you with this endeavor.

Love, Millie

Dear Millie,

For most of my life I've been a straight-A student. Then in junior high, my grades dropped and my parents decided to homeschool me. This is my first year of homeschooling, and now my grades are back up to straight A's. Next year I start high school, and I don't want to miss out. A lot of people have said high school was the best years of their life. My parents want to homeschool me again. I have already proven to them that I can keep up with my grades, but they don't care. They think my friends were the reason for my bad grades, but it's really because I never did my homework. I've told them that, but they don't seem to listen. Please help!

—*Maddie I. (age 14)*

Dear Maddie,

I know this is difficult for you. Both types of education have different benefits and advantages.

I encourage you to pray that God will give your parents wisdom and understanding in making the best decisions for you. Stay patient in this process and submissive to your parents. They have your best interests in mind. Keep talking things over with them. Remember to be respectful. Take a close look at your own motives. How do you hold up spiritually at public school? Are you there for social fun or are you serious about being a witness for Christ?

If you feel that God is calling you to high school and that you're strong enough to stand firm in your faith, then ask your parents if they will give you a chance to prove yourself. Maybe they will be open to a trial run. If after the first semester they are not pleased with your grades, behavior, or attitude, then agree to go back to homeschooling.

Begin now to demonstrate responsible and mature choices, especially with your choice of friends. If the Lord wants you to go to high school, then your parents will feel a peace about it also. Give it to the Lord, Maddie. Even Jesus had to choose to align His will with the Father's in the Garden of Gethsemane (Luke 22:42). Let this also be your prayer: "Not my will, but yours be done." Be at peace and trust God to have His way in this.

Love, Millie

Dear Millie,

God is radically changing my life these days. I'm keeping the Sabbath, making new Christian friends, helping others come to Christ, and just oh so many other wonderful things! I was wondering if you had any tips on how to stay firm for Christ in my public school. I just have this feeling that this year is my year to shine and to change. I have a new look and a new feeling about me that I like and I really believe God is going to use me and my family in powerful ways (my mom is going to be the high school youth group leader at our church). Do you have any suggestions on what to do?

—*Lynn K. (age 13)*

Dear Lynn,

I'm excited for you. It sounds like you're in for a great year at school and church! Since you are feeling a fresh grace on your life to grow stronger and more fruitful, I would encourage you to hold the course. Stay bold and confident that God will use you in many ways. Continue to keep Him the center of your life. Start each day offering yourself to the Lord in prayer, worship, and Bible study. Ask the Holy Spirit to lead you in every situation. Then trust Him to open doors and opportunities for you to be salt and light in your school. You do not need to strive or be anxious, just be full of God! Enjoy Him, rest in Him, and be full of peace and joy. Others will notice something different about you.

Your effectiveness will flow out of abiding in God's Spirit.

You might look closely at John 15. If you really want to be fruitful in the vineyard where God has planted you, you must draw all your sustenance from Christ, the Branch. Closely guard your fellowship with Him. Drink from the Fountain of Life and you will have rivers of living water flowing through you to others. You can easily get burned out if you try to rush out there and save everybody or help everyone with their problems. That's why I want to make sure that you are taking plenty of time to get your spiritual nourishment from Jesus. Your effectiveness will flow out of abiding in God's Spirit. Be prayerful and watchful. Let the Lord guide you to those whose hearts are hungry for Him.

May you be a fruitful vine at your school this year and have a lot of fun doing it!

Love, Millie

I am going to a private Christian school this year, but my family is moving this summer, and I will be going to a public school. I'm a little nervous about how people will treat me when they find out I'm a Christian. Do you have any advice?

—RoseBeth W. (age 14)

Dear RoseBeth,

I understand your nervousness, but try looking at this as an exciting new adventure. Trust that this is God's plan and will for your life. If this is settled in your heart, then you can look ahead with peace and great faith. This doesn't mean it will be easy or that it will go the way you want, but you have the promise that you will be victorious through Christ Jesus (Romans 8:37). Stand strong in your faith! Look ahead with great hope and expectation that God will use you in the public school in a powerful way.

It is also good to remember that persecution is really an expected part of our Christian life. When we walk in righteousness, wickedness will come against us. But we must never fear the persecution, because it will only make us stronger. It actually causes the Kingdom of God to advance. 1 Peter 4:12–19 is a great passage on suffering for Christ.

Finally, I believe that if you are walking in God's love, accepting others, and extending grace and compassion to them, you will be respected and befriended by

Look ahead with great hope .

most. Now, this may take time, so be patient. You have to be willing to walk out your faith in love and let the Spirit of Christ win them over. If you stay trusting God, full of hope, filled with His joy and peace, you will see many hearts open to you.

May the Lord strengthen you and fill you with His confidence to lay hold of the blessings He has for you in this school.

Love, Millie

Dear Millie,

I need help at school. My teacher does not like Christians. The other day he said that the Bible was stupid and he said that the first man was a monkey. When a girl said that she thought Adam was the first human, he said that the Creation was a made-up story and that it wasn't true. I really care about him and I want him to come to know Christ, but it's hard to argue with him because he has a bad temper and he's the teacher! Please help me.

—Persecuted (age 10)

Dear Persecuted,

This is a difficult situation that Christians often face and you are wise to seek counsel about how to respond. Make sure your parents know about the situation and how he is reacting to differing opinions in the classroom.

I'm glad you feel compassion for him. Keep praying for him. I don't think it will do any good to argue with him against evolution. Keep your convictions firm in your heart and ask the Lord to give you opportunities to show him the love of God. God's love will persuade him more than intellectual discussions or arguments. Your kindness toward him will speak louder than any words, and your faithful prayers can soften his heart to hear God's truths.

Ask the Lord to give you opportunities to show him the love of God.

You may enjoy reading some books on Creation as opposed to evolution. You would learn a lot and be more prepared to defend your beliefs.

Thanks for writing. May the Lord give you confidence to stand firm on biblical truth in the face of persecution!

Love, Millie

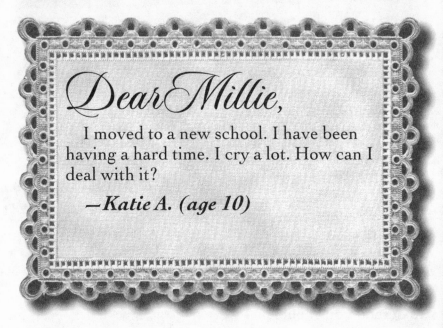

Dear Millie,

I moved to a new school. I have been having a hard time. I cry a lot. How can I deal with it?

—*Katie A. (age 10)*

Dear Katie,

I know how difficult this is for you. You are not alone in your struggle. My move to Pleasant Plains brought a few tears to my own eyes, and I really can understand your hardship. I have heard from many others who have also experienced the difficulty of trying to make the hard transition to a new school. I want to encourage you to hang in there. It will get better—I guarantee it!

It takes time to get adjusted and to make new friends. So be patient with the process. You will not always feel so lonely. In time you will begin to develop good friends. Stay strong in the Lord. Trust Him to give you His perfect peace and strength every day. Be courageous and full of faith. He has not abandoned or forgotten you. Allow this time of hardship to draw you closer to Jesus. He will get you through this, and you will be so much stronger because of it.

Don't forget that every trial has an end. It is just a season and it will soon be over. Let the words spoken to Joshua from the Lord encourage you also. Joshua 1:9 says, "Have I not commanded you? Be strong and courageous. Do not be terrified; do not be discouraged, for the Lord your God will be with you wherever you go." Like Joshua, you are being led into a strange land, but God is with you and He wants you to be strong, not afraid. He will establish you in this new land.

Don't forget that every trial has an end.

Blessings to you, Katie. Hang in there. You're going to be fine.

Love, Millie

Dear Millie,

I have a problem with a friend. We were really close when we were younger, but now all I can think about are her faults — I can't think of any good things about her. Whenever I see her she really annoys me. It seems like I have matured and she hasn't. We don't like any of the same things anymore, and I really don't want to be her friend any longer. How can I tell her without hurting her feelings? Her brother and my brother are really good friends and we see them a lot. She really wants to be my friend. Please help me!

— *Brooke M. (age 11)*

Dear Brooke,

Friendships go through changes like the seasons of our lives. It is natural to want to cultivate new friends as you grow and your interests change. It is likewise just as natural to slowly drift apart from old friends due to these same reasons, but I would caution you against any hasty decisions to cast off an old friend. There is something very beautiful about a friendship you've had for a long time. Don't be so quick to give up on it.

There's an old saying that goes, "Make new friends, but keep the old. One is silver and the other is gold." You do not need to say anything to your friend. It's not worth the risk of hurting her. You always want to keep a bridge between the two of you, because you never know what the future holds. As your friend matures, you may rekindle common interests again.

> *As your friend matures, you may rekindle common interests again.*

For now, relax and just let things take their course. Don't go out of your way to avoid contact with her. Let run-ins happen naturally. Always be very kind and thoughtful toward her. But at the same time, be true to your heart. Pursue other friends you enjoy being with. Ask the Lord to work in the situation, and closely examine your heart to be sure that you are walking in love and compassion, not self-centeredness.

"Do nothing out of selfish ambition or vain conceit, but in humility consider others better than yourselves. Each of you should look not only to your own interests, but also to the interests of others," (Philippians 2:3–4).

Love, Millie

Dear Millie,

I go to middle school and have four best friends. Three of these friends claim themselves as really popular. Sometimes they make fun of people. I know that is wrong, but I don't say anything. They are not Christians like I am. If I speak up, they get mad at me and we end up in a big fight. If I choose not to be their friend, then they will turn half of the school against me. I don't want to go to school having fear about what may happen next. I pray to God that He will help me and it has been a long time. And for some reason I can't hear His voice. So please help me.

—*Valerie G. (age 11)*

Dear Valerie,

You are faced with a decision. Do you want to please God and serve Him with all your heart, or do you want to please men and make everybody like you? Paul said in Galatians 1:10, "Am I now trying to win the approval of men, or of God? Or am I trying to please men? If I were still trying to please men, I would not be a servant of Christ."

If you are sincerely serving God, then you will have to make bold stands against unrighteousness. When your friends are doing something wrong, you can either speak up against it with gentleness and love, or walk away and have nothing to do with it. They will then see that your faith is very serious to you and that you aren't just playing a game. After a while, I believe some of them will come to respect you and desire to know more about Jesus, because they see that you are really different. If they get mad, then they aren't really the kind of friends you want to be hanging with anyway. I seriously doubt if they can turn half the school against you. Do not fear the consequences of doing what is right. God will be with you. "The Lord is with me; I will not be afraid. What can man do to me?" (Psalm 118:6).

I believe you will have more peace and a greater sense of God's presence in your heart when you make the decision to obey and honor Him above all else. Just remember to do all things with love. Love is merciful and compassionate, but also strong and bold for righteousness.

You might also begin to ask the Lord for some really good friends who love Jesus like you do. Stay open to developing new relationships. You don't have to give up your old friends, but you would be greatly blessed to have believing friends also.

Love, Millie

Dear Millie,

My three best friends are moving all at once! One is moving to Texas where I might not see her again. The other two are sisters and they are moving to the desert where I won't see them often. This is really upsetting me. On top of it all, my dad is going to be out of a job soon. Please help!

— *Sad a lot B. (age 11)*

Dear Sad a Lot,

I know the pain of losing three dear friends! I also know the strain of a father losing his job. Because of hard financial times, my family had to move from Ohio to Indiana, and I had to say good-bye to my three best friends. Indeed, you are facing many difficulties. But take heart! God is with you! Every ending is a new beginning.

You must try to look for the blessings and joys that the Lord has in your life right now and focus on them, instead of focusing on the sadness. When I moved away from my friends, it was hard. But God had something special for me (treasures in darkness), and He has something special for you too.

The Scriptures tell us that God allows difficult times in our lives because they are opportunities for us to grow in our faith and trust in God. Romans 5:3–5 says, "We also rejoice in our sufferings, because we know that suffering produces perseverance; perseverance, character; and character, hope. And hope does not disappoint us, because God has poured out his love into our hearts by the Holy Spirit, whom he has given us."

Even in hard times God is at work around you.

Gain comfort from these words and really embrace the thought that God truly has a deep love for you, your family, and friends. Times might be hard right now, but allow the Father to carry you through. Like I said, turn your thoughts to the blessings in your life when you find yourself overcome with sadness. I also encourage you to be open to meeting new people and making new friends. Pray and ask God to guide you to new friends, and a new job for your Father.

Even in hard times God is at work around you. Use this challenging time to grow in your friendship with Jesus. He is with you always!

Love, Millie

Dear Millie,

I have no friends! It's so painful to see girls my age at church ignore me, and everything I say! Can you help me? Do you know of any programs for girls my age (11-13)? I don't go to school and that makes it harder. How did you make friends? All my "friends" talk about boys and boring "junk!"

—Ellie E. (age 11)

Dear Ellie,

I'm sorry you are feeling ignored by girls at church. One thing that helps me when I begin to feel lonely is to look around and see who God has brought into my life that really love me. Consider your parents, cousins, siblings, and aunts and uncles who love you and support you. Then next thing you can do is to think if there is anyone in your life who also could use a new friend. Maybe there are other girls in your church who

feel left out or who sit alone. Try reaching out to someone new. Who knows! This could be your new best
friend!

The Lord can use you to share His love with someone. Maybe it's time to reach out and develop some
new friendships. You could also consider attending
your church's youth group or
youth Bible study. Perhaps you

*Maybe it's time to reach
out and develop some
new friendships.*

could join the choir or a theater
group to meet new friends. There
are many opportunities out there
for girls your age. You just have
to begin looking for them and be open to try something
new. Just remember that Jesus is truly the best friend
you can have. So press into Him and trust Him to lead
you to a friend!

Love, Millie

Dear Millie,

A lot of my friends are going to different middle schools. I'm homeschooled and feel sort of left out of it. There's a part of my friends' lives that I don't know anything about. They are starting to wear makeup (I don't), and they carry purses (I don't). I don't get invited to as many parties as I used to. They don't talk about the parties, but it doesn't take a brain to figure out they go to them. I would rather have them talk about the parties than make it a big secret. The problem is, I'm afraid of change. I want them to be my best friends for life. I'm afraid someone will take them all away.

—*Noelle C. (age 12)*

Dear Noelle,

I understand how you feel. Change is scary because it is unfamiliar. Change may mean things don't go the way you want. It is hard to look at a future full of changes without trusting God. You must believe that God loves you and promises never to leave you.

It may not be the way you want it at first, but if you surrender yourself to God, you have chosen to live your life for God's purposes and not your own. You can therefore rest in the loving arms of God and accept with perfect peace what comes into your life. Give these concerns about your friends to the Lord. He knows what is best. If they are truly friends that He wants you to have, they will be yours. Don't feel pressured to have to change to be like them or even to have the same experiences as they do. It is very important for you to be yourself. Give your friends a chance. Be honest with them about your feelings. Let God bring you the friends who will accept you and encourage you in your walk with the Lord.

> *Give these concerns about your friends to the Lord.*

Hold on to the Lord. He is a solid place to stand on in the midst of a constantly changing world.

Love, Millie

Dear Millie,

I have a friend who is very loud and noisy. I don't like being around her even though she is a wonderful Christian girl. It seems like every one else likes her except me. How can I get over this? I didn't invite her to my last birthday party because I didn't want to be around her. I hurt her feelings a lot and I am sorry, but I still don't like playing with her. She has 3 brothers and no sisters so that makes me feel like I need to like her even more. Please help me.

— *Confused B. (age 13)*

Dear Confused,

We all have people in our lives who are harder to love than others. You do not have to be close friends with everybody, but you do need to love everybody. Love comes from God. Ask God to help you see her the way He does. Ask Him for more compassion and sensitivity to her needs and struggles. Ask God to change your heart and fill you with His love.

You may never really be a close friend to her, but when you are with her, you will have grace to be patient, kind, and loving. Through your prayers for her, she may begin to change, and you could find her to be a lot of fun after all. Don't forget that you have your own flaws, and you want people to be patient with you and merciful to you.

You do not have to be close friends with everybody, but you do need to love everybody.

Love, Millie

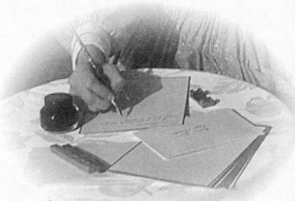

Dear Millie,

I've always been very close to my cousin, even though she's four years older than I am, but lately she's been acting really strange. She talks to me about stuff she does and makes me promise not to tell anyone. I think she might be doing drugs and I'm scared for her. What can I do to help her?

— *Audri P. (age 11)*

Dear Audri,

It is good you have a close relationship with your cousin, but be very careful, especially since she is four years older. She is possibly sharing things that are inappropriate for you. Don't let anybody force you into a promise of secrecy. Some things are too heavy for you to bear alone and it is not always best for that person to keep everything undercover anyway. Read Ephesians 5:11–14 as it may apply to this situation. Do not lend an ear to the dark side. Keep yourself in the light by staying really open with your parents about your concerns for your cousin and your conversations.

It's hard to help somebody who doesn't want help. Your cousin may be totally happy with the way things are. God has given you His love and compassion for her. Turn it into strong, faith-filled prayer, and let your life be a witness of God's love and purity. Continue to be loving, kind, and yet speaking truth when necessary. Pray for an opportunity to boldly share about Jesus and what He can do for her. Don't give up believing that she is going to be saved. I am believing with you.

Some things are too heavy for you to bear alone.

Love, Millie

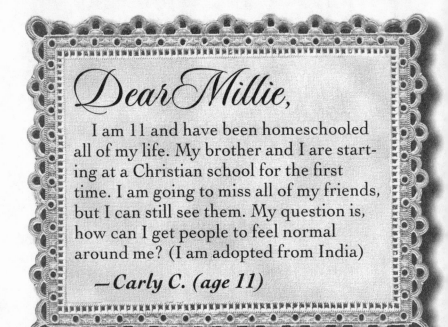

Dear Millie,

I am 11 and have been homeschooled all of my life. My brother and I are starting at a Christian school for the first time. I am going to miss all of my friends, but I can still see them. My question is, how can I get people to feel normal around me? (I am adopted from India)

—Carly C. (age 11)

Dear Carly,

It sounds like you are going to begin a new adventure in your life. I like to look at changes that way—as adventures. They certainly can be rather frightening because everything is different and you don't know what to expect. But if you face it as a challenge, which you know will only cause you to grow, you can be optimistic about it. Commit it to the Lord and begin to trust that He is with you and will work all things out for your good (Romans 8:28).

To answer your question about your adoption, I believe much of what you think people are feeling about you depends on how you feel about yourself. In other words, are you secure in who you are? Are you okay with your adoption? I really believe that if you are relaxed and comfortable around people and not self-conscious about being from India, you will find that people will be comfortable with you. The battle is within you, not with others. Adoption is very common-place in our country. Our nation is full of foreigners who call America their home. You are one of many. Settle things in your heart. Know without a shadow of doubt that God planned and purposed your life. Be totally confident in His perfect love and acceptance for you. Receive this and be at peace within. You will then be at peace with others and it will not even matter to you what they are thinking.

> *If you belong to the body of Christ, there are no distinctions as to race, gender, or ethnic group.*

Thanks for writing, Carly. May you find complete joy and peace in who you are in Jesus. If you belong to the body of Christ, there are no distinctions as to race, gender, or ethnic group (Galatians 3:26–28).

Love, Millie

Dear Millie,

There is a new girl in my homeroom who just moved here from Korea. I think there is a good chance she is a Buddhist. At lunch I asked her what type of religion they have in Korea. She just said "all kinds" and seemed not to want to talk about it. How can I try to lead her to Christ without offending her?

—*Betsie H. (age 13)*

Dear Betsie,

What a wonderful thing to have a friend from another country! I think it is even more exciting for you to get to share your faith with her.

It starts with a friendship, though. Just get to know her. You don't want to start right out with really deep issues. You can certainly tell her about yourself and about your church, but avoid asking direct questions until you know she really feels comfortable with you. It takes time to develop trust with someone. She will be watching you closely. Your actions and speech will be your starting place for sharing Jesus. Be faithful to live your life demonstrating the love of Christ. In time as you get to know each other more, you can invite her to your church or a youth group activity. These things will naturally encourage questions from her or opportunities for you to share more with her. Go slowly; never be pushy. Make it your aim to love her, accept her, and serve her. Regularly pray for the Holy Spirit to open her heart to receive the truth of the Gospel.

> *Make it your aim to love her, accept her, and serve her.*

I'm so pleased that you have such a love and compassion for this girl. I'm sure she is feeling very lonely and possibly frightened. It is a big adjustment adapting to a different culture and not knowing anybody. She will need a good friend and I'm so glad you are the one God has picked. May you grow to be great friends and someday share together the greatest Friend of all!

Love, Millie

Dear Millie,

I live in Turkey and all my friends are non-Christians except for one. I would like them to become Christians. Do you have any suggestions? I also go to public school. They have Muslim classes, but I don't do them. Sometimes they even tease me about it. What should I do?

—*Renee I. (age 11)*

Dear Renee,

It's so good to hear from you. I think God has divinely put you in a very exciting place. What an adventure you're on! I know there are hard times in every adventure, like when the girls tease you. But remember the persecution Jesus went through and let Him give you strength.

1 Peter 4:12–19 will encourage you when you feel persecuted. Don't take their teasing too seriously—just keep loving them and letting your light shine. I'm so

glad you have a Christian friend to encourage you. You two can really have great times of prayer and fellowship together.

The best way to show these girls Jesus is to let them feel His love through you. When they see the effects of His love on your life — your peace, joy, kindness, etc. — they will know that you have something very special and they will begin to ask about it. Then *You are planting seeds.* you will have many wonderful opportunities to share about Jesus. Be patient with the process. You are planting seeds. God will see to it that they are watered and He will cause the growth.

Keep yourself rooted in God's Word, prayer, and worship. May you be a fruitful branch in this wonderful mission field.

Love, *Millie*

Dear Millie,

I have an adopted little sister. She can be a little annoying, but I still love her. But my dad is usually really mean to her. He acts as if he doesn't even like her! I try to help her out, but what else can I do? I'm supposed to respect my parents, but how can I tell my dad he's wrong in what he does?

— *Troubled (age 15)*

Dear Troubled,

I'm so glad that you are kind to your little sister. It sounds like she could really use your love and comfort.

I think you should pray about speaking with your father. It may be helpful that your mother is present when you do. It is not disrespectful to be honest about something that is bothering you, as long as you do it with respect and in the right way. Don't tell him he's doing something wrong. Go to him with your feelings. Tell him that sometimes the way he treats your adopted sister upsets and hurts you deeply. You could ask him if there is anything you could do to help him understand her better or to be more patient with her. Tell him you are concerned for her emotional well-being. I know this may be scary, because you are afraid of upsetting him, but I think it's worth a try. It will make him think about it. He may be unaware of how his behavior is affecting you and your sister.

Pray for God to fill your family with His love.

Hopefully, he will soften toward your little sister.

Make sure you are praying about the situation. Ask for grace and wisdom before you talk with your father. Pray for God to fill your family with His love. It might help to speak with your mother or another trusted adult first to seek other counsel.

May God give you boldness to speak the truth in love on behalf of your precious little sister.

Love, Millie

Dear Millie,

My older brother moved away from home a few years ago and now he has a girlfriend who is not a Christian. He used to be a Christian when he lived at home, but since he moved away he doesn't want to have anything to do with God. The relationship seems to be serious and now he is even going to move in with her. I love him, but lately I have been feeling really angry with him and I don't want to have anything to do with him. What should I do?

— *Claire P. (age 13)*

Dear Claire,

I understand your anger. You deeply love your brother and care for him, and it hurts you to see him turning from God. Take your feelings to the Lord and let Him comfort you. At the same time, keep praying for your brother's restoration to the Lord. Pray in faith and entrust him to the Lord. You can't change your brother. Only God can soften his heart back to the truth.

Withdrawing from your brother out of anger is damaging to your relationship with him and will hinder God from using you in his life. Your brother needs to see the unconditional love of God, which is not influenced by his behavior. He needs to know that no matter what he does, you will love him. At the same time, having assured him of your commitment to him, you also have an obligation to speak truth to him. It's okay to tell him that you are very grieved about some of the choices he's making right now. Tell him you love him enough to want the best for him and you know that best is Jesus. Let him know that you are committed to pray for him and his relationship with God.

> *Be patient and persevering in prayer.*

After you have spoken your heart, don't keep nagging him. Prove your commitment to love him no matter what, and trust God to give you opportunities to encourage him in the Lord. Be patient and persevering in prayer. God will answer, but it may take a long time (possibly years!). Don't give up hope, just keep believing.

"Be devoted to one another in brotherly love. Honor one another above yourselves. . . . Be joyful in hope, patient in affliction, faithful in prayer" (Romans 12:10, 12).

Love, Millie

Dear Millie,

My mom and dad got divorced four years ago. My mom is remarried, but my brother does not like the man my mom married. My dad doesn't either. I am being put in the middle of it all. I like him but I keep hearing bad stuff about him. It's hard to like him. Now my dad is getting married. What if the same thing happens again?

—Gina W. (age 9)

Dear Gina,

You have been through a lot for a 9-year-old! God must have great plans to make you a strong woman of God. The most important thing I would like to encourage you with is, "Don't be afraid." Just because you've gone through a lot of trials doesn't mean it's always going to be hard. Things do get better, and God has a plan for your future, which is full of hope. "There is surely a future hope for you, and your hope will not be cut off," promises Proverbs 23:18. So, keep your faith completely in God and His goodness and don't look back. Tomorrow is a new day!

Next, a word of encouragement: Be a peacemaker. If you can develop good relationships with your parents' new spouses, it will make things more peaceful for you and the rest of your family. "God has called us to live in peace," says 1 Corinthians 7:15. You do not have to be forced in the middle. Let your

You can be a ray of sunshine.

parents know that you love them and that you intend to live in peace with their new spouses. Allowing contention, bitterness, or unforgiveness to exist will hinder the healing and redeeming process that God wants to do in your family. There has already been enough damage done. It's time to build again.

You are definitely in a challenging place, but it is not outside of God's abundant grace. You can be a ray of sunshine to them that brings the much-needed mercy and forgiveness of God into their lives.

May the Lord fill you with joy and peace as you trust in Him.

Love, Millie

Dear Millie,

Our whole family wants my aunt to get saved. If you talk about anything that has to do with the Bible, she gets aggressive. We have prayed to the Lord about her, but He hasn't answered in a way that I know of. She has a daughter who is four years old, and is a real brat. Whenever her mom asks her to do anything, she says NO, NO, NO! She is so disobedient! What should I do? I desperately want her to receive Christ, but why is it SO hard?

— *Angela R. (age 10)*

Dear Angela,

I appreciate your compassion and burden for your aunt's salvation. This is the heart of God. Remember, though, it is God's burden. Let Him carry it for you. Stay faithful to pray for her and be very patient. God will change her in His perfect time. It may take years. Just because you don't see anything happening does not mean God is not working. We cannot see how powerful our prayers are and what is being done in the heavenlies. So do not waver in your faith for her salvation.

Since she gets defensive when you talk about the Bible, I would avoid such discussions. Just seek to love her and her daughter unconditionally. Demonstrate to them the love of Jesus. She knows how you believe and she probably knows what to believe, but her heart has not yet

Do not waver in your faith for her salvation.

been touched. Until that happens, respect and accept where she is and seek to be a blessing to her. Let the Spirit of Christ minister to her through you.

If her daughter is with you and acts inappropriately, it is good for you to firmly, yet lovingly, correct and instruct her. I don't think your aunt will mind if she sees how much you love her.

God wants to teach you much through this. May you find great joy in allowing God to use you as a vessel to demonstrate His love and compassion for your aunt. You will find yourself maturing in your own walk with the Lord.

I will pray in agreement with you for your aunt's salvation.

Love, Millie

Dear Millie,

I am going through a very difficult time right now. My parents are getting divorced. I have three brothers that are constantly bothering me about certain things, and to make matters worse, I don't have any friends that I can talk to. I'm the only girl in my family, and my parents are always busy. I don't know what to do. Sometimes I feel that God does not love me, although I know I shouldn't. It's just so hard. I don't have anybody to talk to.

—Danielle J. (age 11)

Dear Danielle,

You are definitely going through a difficult time and really do need someone to talk to. I urge you to confide in a trusted adult at your church or in your family (like an aunt). It doesn't have to be a friend of your own age. Don't be afraid to ask for help.

Also, go to your mom or dad and tell them how lonely and scared you feel. They won't know you're hurting if you don't tell them. Even though they seem busy, I'm sure you are a big priority to them. When you keep your fears and hurts trapped inside, Satan begins to lie to you. He will tell you that nobody cares for you and that even God doesn't care for you. Talking about your feelings to them will diminish these lies and will give you a new perspective on the situation.

Your brothers might have the same feelings about the divorce as you. Consider sharing with them how you're feeling; they may open up also. When you understand how they are hurting, you will have compassion and patience for them. Everybody handles pain differently. Your brothers may seem buggy and bothersome because of their own pain. Ask God for the grace to love them. Draw strength and encouragement from one another during this time, instead of letting this stressful situation cause you to turn against each other.

Finally, God does know everything that is going on with you, and He does care! 1 Peter 5:7 says to cast your cares on Him because He cares for you. Even though it looks dark right now, and you feel your prayers aren't being answered, KNOW that God sees it all and cares very deeply. He will give you the grace you need to get through each day.

May God be your rock in the midst of the storm. Cling to Him and you will be safe. He will see you through.

Love, Millie

Dear Millie,

At home my dad calls me stupid and gets mad at almost every wrong thing I do. When I wash the dishes for my mom he tells me that I don't know how to wash them. If I don't practice my piano long enough he yells at me and says I will never get anywhere with my life. If I go to college I have to study what HE wants me to study. It makes me feel like I am not worth a penny, either in God's sight or my dad's. I cry all the time and I write a lot in my diary, but it isn't the same as telling someone. Please help!

—Hurt So Bad (age 14)

Dear Hurt So Bad,

I'm so glad you opened your heart to me, and I am so sorry for what you are going through. God knows your pain and He sees your father's unkind behavior. You must believe that Jesus is the great Redeemer and that

He loves you. Trust Him and surrender the whole thing to Him.

Take refuge in the Lord. The Psalms are full of heart-wrenching prayers for God to deliver and save. Comb the Psalms and find the verses that you can use as prayers and write them down. Let the Lord spread His wings over you and comfort you (Zephaniah 3:17). Take all your hurts and sorrows to the loving arms of your Heavenly Father. He has comfort to give you.

Pray for your father. He needs to receive God's love for himself. His actions probably reflect the pain and hurt in his own heart. Ask God to protect you from getting bitter against him (Colossians 3:13).

Also consider writing an honest letter to your father. Affirm your love and respect for him as your father, but ask him to please consider what you are saying. You may be afraid of angering him, and I understand this. So be careful. But know too that fear is not of God. Don't let fear keep you from doing what is right. Pray and seek counsel before you write the letter. If it is written with love and respect, he should be able to receive it. Pray that God would turn this situation around and bring a wonderful restoration between you and your father.

Before you do anything, bathe it in prayer and ask for God's help and guidance. I am praying for you. Keep your chin up, and your eyes on your Savior. Don't be afraid. He is with you. Nothing in all creation can separate you from God's love (Romans 8:39).

Love, Millie

Dear Millie,

My family is going through some difficult times right now. We are having bad money problems and my parents don't seem to be telling me what's going on. I mean, I didn't figure out that my dad had cancer till about a month after they found out (thank God he is cured now). How can I ask God to help us with our money problem without sounding selfish? Also, how can I get my parents to talk to me about what is going on? Please help me!

— *Ivy T. (age 10)*

Dear Ivy,

I'm sure your parents are trying to shield you from things that might needlessly worry or upset you. They probably don't realize that you can sense the tension, and that you have picked up on some of the problems your family is facing. You must be honest with them about how you feel. At the same time, trust their discernment to give you only the information you need.

Never hesitate taking any concerns you have to God. It is not selfish to pray for anything that is on your heart. Money problems are very stressful for a family, and God can bring relief, so by all means pray. Philippians 4:6 says, "Do not be anxious about ANYTHING, but in EVERYTHING, by prayer and petition, with thanksgiving, present your requests to God."

> *Never hesitate taking any concerns you have to God.*

Go to your Heavenly Father with your concerns and receive all you need there.

Love, Millie

Dear Millie,

My mom will not let me get e-mail or instant messaging. I only have truly saved friends and I would have NO desire to start a friendship with an unsaved person. I've learned it is no use begging or pleading once my mom makes a rule or says no. It gets me so mad and I get a few rebellious thoughts. The Bible says to obey your parents but I get mad every time I think of what my mom said. How can I fully submit?

—*Upset R. (age 12)*

Dear Upset,

It is normal when you experience frustration, anger, and rebellious feelings toward your parents. We will always be tempted with bad thoughts and feelings, but this is not a sin. Remember, even Jesus was tempted.

The flesh will always resist when it doesn't get its way, as you have experienced with the e-mail and instant messaging. But this is where you have to win the battle. If you give in to the bad, rebellious thoughts and allow them to linger, it will affect your behavior. You will begin to act out what you are thinking about. So it would be wise to accept the verdict your mother has given for now. Fight your rebellious, angry thoughts with God's Word.

Use Ephesians 6:1–3, and 1 Peter 5:6, "Humble yourselves, therefore, under God's mighty hand, that he may lift you up in due time." Look at this as being the restraining hand of God and not just your mom and dad. God will make a way for His will in your life. Submit it to Him. Trust that He is working through your parents' decision for what is best for you. Do not lean on your own understanding (Proverbs 3:5).

> *Fight your rebellious, angry thoughts with God's Word.*

Maybe in six months or a year you can respectfully ask your parents to reconsider their position. Ask them if they will give you a chance to prove to be trustworthy with the privilege. Your humility now will make a way for God to allow you favor with this in the future.

For now, just release it to the Lord. Humble yourself under His authority and that of your parents. By doing this, you will receive the fullness of God's blessing in your life, which is of more value to you than any e-mail or instant messaging ever could be.

Love, Millie

Dear Millie,

My father has a really crazy work schedule! Sometimes he can be gone for a whole week. I don't know how to deal with my—I have to say—hatred toward his job. I am grateful he has a job; just sometimes I wish he had a less busy schedule. Could you please help me?

—*Victoria V. (age 12)*

Dear Victoria,

I certainly understand how you feel. I know you wish you could spend more time with your father. You can certainly pray that God would give your dad a job where he could be home more. But until that happens, if ever, you must accept things the way they are and make the most out of them; getting upset or even complaining about our circumstances does no good. What you need to do is maximize the times you are with your dad. Make every moment count. Quality time is just as important as quantity.

Don't forget to pray a lot for your dad. I'm sure it's just as hard on him to be away from his family. Don't forget to focus on all the things you have to be thankful for. You have a dad who loves you. This in itself is a major blessing that many girls do not have.

Quality time is just as important as quantity.

"Always giving thanks to God the Father for everything, in the name of our Lord Jesus Christ" (Ephesians 5:20).

Love, Millie

Dear Millie,

I'll be a teenager in 2 months and I've heard a lot about "rebellious teens" and how it's just something that happens at my age. I'm trying hard not to be that way, but I get so angry at my parents for not letting me do things that I think I should be able to do. They treat me like a child and make me feel like my best is not good enough. It seems like they can't trust me. My parents are good Christians, but I feel misunderstood.

—*Missy C. (age 12)*

Dear Missy,

You are at an awkward age where you are beginning to blossom into a young woman, and yet in many ways you are still a child. You are quickly changing physically and emotionally. It is easy to feel misunderstood, and it is normal to want more freedom to stretch your wings.

You are very blessed to have Christian parents who are seeking the Lord and praying for wisdom. This should make it easier for you to trust that God will reveal His will for you through them. Even if you disagree with their decisions, God is watching to see if you will still trust Him and submit.

Communication between teens and parents is so important. If you feel like you are being treated like a child, talk with your parents about it. Let them know specifically where you would like

Set a standard of holiness for your generation.

to have more involvement in decision-making. If you stay patient and respectful, the three of you can come to compromises that make everybody happy. Guard your heart against any form of rebellion and God will bless you for it. Remember the promise in Ephesians 6:1–3—It will go well with those who obey the commandment to honor your father and mother.

It is a grave deception for people to say that it is normal and expected for teenagers to rebel. That is not God's plan for young people nor should it ever be expected. God's plan for young people is that they walk in His purity, power, and strength, totally submitted to the God-given authority in their lives. This is God's heart for young people today. May you set a standard of holiness for your generation.

Love, Millie

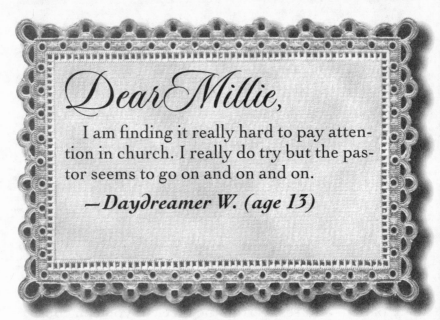

Dear Millie,

I am finding it really hard to pay attention in church. I really do try but the pastor seems to go on and on and on.

—*Daydreamer W. (age 13)*

Dear Daydreamer,

At one time or another we all struggle with staying focused during church. Remember when Jesus was praying in the Garden of Gethsemane before He was arrested? He asked His disciples to stay and sit with Him, but they kept falling asleep. He said to them, "Watch and pray so that you will not fall into temptation. The spirit is willing, but the body is weak" (Matthew 26:41). I know you have a willing spirit; you are just struggling with what the Bible calls "your flesh," or the weakness of your human body and will.

If your parents don't mind, try some of these suggestions when your attention begins to wander: Bring a notebook with you so that you can take notes on the sermon. This may help you stay focused. If you get too bored with that, have your Bible handy so you can do some of your own reading. This is a wonderful way to redeem the time. Use your notebook to journal anything God shows you in your reading. Get your prayer list out (or make one) and have a wonderful time of prayer. Or look around the room and pray for people you see who have specific needs. These activities will be useful in keeping your spirit strong and you will not have squandered precious time on just daydreaming. Refer back to Jesus' admonition to His disciples in the garden: "Watch and pray so that you will not fall into temptation."

> *"Watch and pray so that you will not fall into temptation."*

"Be very careful, then, how you live. . . making the most of every opportunity, because the days are evil," says Ephesians 5:15–16.

May your Sunday mornings be a wonderful time of refreshing and spiritual growth for you.

Love, Millie

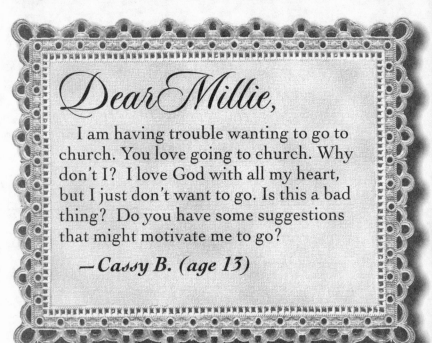

Dear Millie,

I am having trouble wanting to go to church. You love going to church. Why don't I? I love God with all my heart, but I just don't want to go. Is this a bad thing? Do you have some suggestions that might motivate me to go?

— Cassy B. (age 13)

Dear Cassy,

I really appreciate your honesty. I think maybe you find church boring. Many people, youth and adults alike, struggle with this. But I do have a solution—you can find a place to serve in your church.

Church is important for spiritual growth, fellowship with other believers, worship, and many other activities that the body of Christ shares together, such as Communion. These are all wonderful things that strengthen our faith and connect us with other

Bored With Church

Christians. But if we only go to receive, then we will become bored and our faith will stagnate.

I would like to challenge you to find a way to serve at your church on Sunday mornings. Talk to your parents, pastor, or another church staff person about the possibilities for you. Here are a few areas you can prayerfully consider: nursery, Sunday school, helping the elderly, greeting people, hospitality, etc.

> *When you are giving and serving, there is not room for boredom.*

Ask the Lord to open a door for you to use your gifts at church. When you are giving and serving, there is not room for boredom. This is true with our Christian lives also. If we are only receiving and never giving, we will lose our joy and zeal for God. James 2:14–26 tells us that our Christian walk must consist of faith and deeds.

As you serve, you will make friends, meet new people, and find yourself very fulfilled. I pray that you will begin to look forward to Sunday mornings where you can use your gift to serve the body of Christ.

Love, Millie

Dear Millie,

I would love to become a Christian! You see, I'm not very good with relationships, and every time I try and become one, I just forget all about praying and reading my Bible. I would just LOVE to become one of God's children. Could you please give me some suggestions on what to do about it?

—Hannah B. (age 11)

Dear Hannah,

I'm so pleased that you already love the Lord! I want you to understand that your salvation is a love-relationship and is a gift received by believing in Jesus as your Lord and Savior. You don't have to earn God's love by praying and reading your Bible.

As you grow to love God more and more, you will want to talk with Him and read His Word, but this

does not make Him love us more. It just helps us grow
closer to Him. So don't neglect these things, but at the
same time, understand that you
won't lose your salvation because
you forget to have your devotions. I pray that the Holy Spirit
will help you understand and
enjoy the grace of God and His
unconditional love. May you fall in love with Him
more and more each day.

> *You don't have to earn God's love by praying and reading your Bible.*

Love, Millie

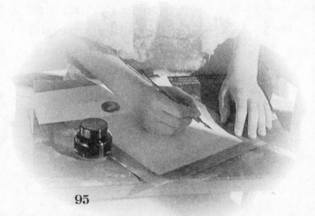

Dear Millie,

I have begun to wonder if I am really a Christian. I am at the point where I can't enjoy myself because I am worried about dying or Jesus' return and not going to heaven. How can I know if I was sincere when accepting Jesus? I have gotten into the habit of asking Jesus into my heart every time I feel unsure. I know it's not about a prayer—it's about my heart. I am trying to trust what God's Word says about salvation instead of what I am feeling. But lately I've been thinking about heaven and hell, and sometimes I get really scared that I'm going to go to hell. I do believe that I can't save myself and that I need Jesus to save me—that's why He died. I've confessed Jesus with my mouth, and I've decided to follow Him, but I still feel insecure. Do you have any thoughts on this?

—Julie L. (age 14)

Dear Julie,

I'm so glad you have written. You must forever settle in your heart the assurance of your salvation so that you can move on in your faith and mature. Otherwise, Satan will continue to torment you with these doubts, and eventually cause you to fall away.

Our salvation is based totally on believing. Here are some Scriptures I want you to read. John 1:12 says, "Yet to all who received him, to those who **believed** in his name, he gave the right to become children of God." See also John 3:16 and John 5:24.

God has said that you have salvation through receiving and believing in His Son Jesus Christ. Now all you have to do is simply take God at His Word. It is done. You are saved by your faith — not on how you feel. You are saved because God has said it. Settle it now and forever, and never doubt it again. It's so simple, isn't it? God has done everything needed for us to be saved and restored to Him through Jesus. All we have to do is believe!

When the doubts come (and they will), you must recognize that Satan is trying to make you stumble. Take the passages above and use them as a weapon against these doubts. We are in a spiritual battle. It is very real, and we must learn how to fight. Only you can fight the enemy of your soul. God has given you everything you need. Rise up, take up the sword of faith (God's Word), and send the devil fleeing!

Love, Millie

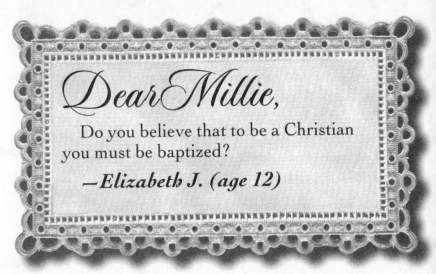

Dear Millie,

Do you believe that to be a Christian you must be baptized?

—*Elizabeth J. (age 12)*

Dear Elizabeth,

If you search the Scriptures, you will see that Jesus commands baptism in the great commission (Matthew 28: 19). Jesus himself was baptized, and the teaching of baptism is mentioned in several places in the New Testament (Romans 6:3–4 and Colossians 2:12).

The book of Acts is full of accounts of believers getting baptized. Therefore I believe baptism is a very important part of our commitment to the Lord Jesus.

Some church denominations may have a different understanding of baptism. You may want to discuss this with your pastor to learn what your church believes. You could do your own study on baptism and see what God shows you. Read all the passages you can find in the New Testament on baptism. Ask the Holy Spirit to help you properly understand as you study. You will learn the truth as you study on your own and lean into the wisdom of those in authority over you.

Thanks for writing.

Love, Millie

Jesus himself was baptized, and the teaching of baptism is mentioned in several places in the New Testament.

Dear Millie,

I like to read your books. I just got my sister to start reading the first book. The books I've read say that you knew many verses. As for me, I only know a few. Right now I'm working on memorizing Psalm 103. How do you memorize? I started Psalm 103 a long time ago and I've only memorized a couple verses.

—*Rachel R. (age 11)*

Dear Rachel,

I'm so thrilled you want to memorize God's Word! You will never regret the effort you put into it. You will have these verses in your mind to draw from for the rest of your life. Also, memorizing comes so much easier at your age. So keep it up! Nothing worthwhile comes easy, you know.

Psalm 103 is a great Psalm to memorize, but it is long. You could do it all at once, but it might be easier to break it down into small bite-size pieces. Set reason-able goals. For instance, try to memorize two verses a week. At the end of that week, add these two verses to the rest and make sure you can say them altogether. When I memorize, I write the verses down on note cards and then I post them on my mirror or carry them in my purse. I keep reading them over and over again. Make sure you are memorizing from a translation of the Bible that you understand.

> *You will never regret the effort you put into it.*

Always record all the Scriptures you have memorized in your journal or notebook so that you can regularly go back over them. This helps you retain them long term and may only need to be done once a month.

We have a journal, *Millie's Daily Diary: A Personal Journal for Girls*, which has eight different tabbed sections for you to write in. One of those sections is called "Scripture Memory & Study." This would be an excellent place for you to keep track of verses you are memorizing.

In Psalm 119:11, David said, "I have hidden your word in my heart that I might not sin against you." This tells us that God's Word can actually guard our hearts. So keep up the good work. You will reap a great reward.

Love, Millie

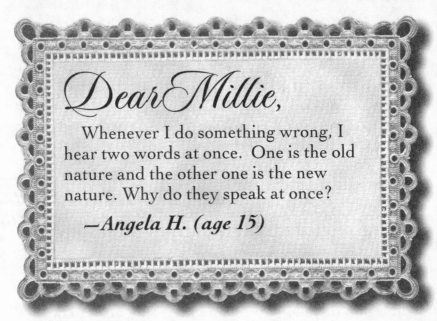

Dear Millie,

Whenever I do something wrong, I hear two words at once. One is the old nature and the other one is the new nature. Why do they speak at once?

—*Angela H. (age 15)*

Dear Angela,

Your question is very insightful and shows that you have understanding about the spiritual battle that goes on in your mind. Paul speaks clearly of this battle in Romans 7:21–25. I strongly urge you to read and study this passage for better understanding of the old and new natures.

The two voices you hear are your old nature and the Holy Spirit (the new life inside of you). Both are speaking. You must decide which voice you will obey. As you grow stronger in God's Spirit, you will have more grace to overcome your old sin nature. Remember, you are going to sin because no one is sinless except Jesus. But eventually, through confession, repentance, and believing God's Word, you will be victorious over that sin!

If you have taken Jesus as your Lord and Savior, you have taken on the life of Christ. His life in you has set you free from the old self, which is under the law of sin and death. It doesn't mean you will never sin. You will be tempted by the old self to keep sinning, but you now have the power through Jesus to overcome. You must believe by faith that Christ's power will help you in your struggle against sin. This is a process that you will walk out the rest of your Christian life.

You must decide which voice you will obey.

Do not lose heart. Keep fighting the fight! Study Romans 7 and ask the Holy Spirit to give you understanding. We are truly in a battle, but as Christ's beloved, you are a valiant, victorious warrior!

Love, Millie

Dear Millie,

I know the Lord is coming soon but I'm sort of scared about it. I'm a Christian and Christians should look forward to it. What if I yell at my sister and then the Lord comes and I'm not ready? The Bible says in the last days perilous times will come and we are already seeing that. I know the Lord's in control but how can I stop being afraid?

—Fearful P. (age 12)

Dear Fearful,

I certainly understand the reality of your struggle against fear. Fear will become prevalent as the disasters and wars increase in our world. But for those in Christ, there will arise a confidence and assurance in their salvation. Remember, God gives us grace for whatever happens to us minute by minute. We cannot begin to comprehend the strength and comfort that

God will supply to us when we need it, so don't try to speculate how you will manage in certain trials or tragedies.

Through Jesus, each day we can "approach the throne of grace with confidence, so that we may receive mercy and find grace to help us in our time of need" (Hebrews 4:16). Live each day in complete trust and faith in God. That's what Jesus was trying to communicate in Matthew 6 when he was teaching the people to trust God for their daily needs and not to worry about the future.

> *Live each day in complete trust and faith in God.*

If you are living each day for Jesus, obeying Him as much as you know how, loving Him with all your heart, soul, mind, and strength, then you will be ready when He returns. This doesn't mean that you will be living perfectly. You will be sinning and making mistakes up until He returns, but His blood cleanses you continually if your heart is turned toward Him. So be bold, confident, and anxiously awaiting the return of our Lord Jesus.

Love, Millie

Dear Millie,

I don't like hearing about the "End Times" and how close we are to it. I want to live my life. I am not afraid of the rapture or going to heaven; it's just the forever part that scares me. The fact that it will never end seems frightening to me. I know it should make me happy, but it doesn't. I don't want to die and I don't want to go to hell or stay on earth after the rapture. I love God with all my heart. When I tell my family about this they just don't seem to understand me.

— *Trista R. (age 13)*

Dear Trista,

I don't think you are alone in feeling this way. It is normal for us to fear the unknown. Eternity ("forever") and death are certainly beyond our human understanding, but so are many other things God talks about in His Word. Humans do not have perfect understanding. Maybe God has kept it that way so we will learn to trust Him. That's where your faith comes in. Jesus is the same yesterday, today, and tomorrow (Hebrews 13:8). The same loving, faithful Savior who guided you into a saving relationship with God, who daily provides for your every need, will be the same for the unknown future. If you can trust Him today for your salvation, then you can trust Him for the fulfillment of that salvation (living forever with Him).

Here's what Jesus told the disciples about eternity: "Do not let your hearts be troubled. Trust in God; trust also in me. In my Father's house are many rooms; if it were not so, I would have told you. I am going there to prepare a place for you. And if I go and prepare a place for you, *I will come back and take you to be with me that you also may be where I am*" (John 14:1–3).

Be encouraged! Jesus will take us with Him. We will be in His arms, never left alone. How can we fear anything if Jesus promises to be with us? In Hebrews 13:5, God promises to never leave us nor forsake us. Do you believe His promises? You can trust Him with your earthly life. You can trust Him with your eternity.

May these Scriptures offer you more peace: 1 Thessalonians 5:9–10; 1 Thessalonians 4:17; 1 Corinthians 2:9.

Get ready for unspeakable joy! In the meantime, live a life of faith!

Love, Millie

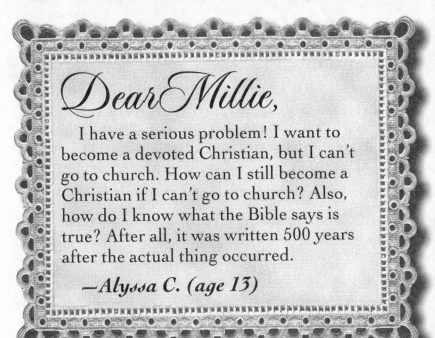

Dear Millie,

I have a serious problem! I want to become a devoted Christian, but I can't go to church. How can I still become a Christian if I can't go to church? Also, how do I know what the Bible says is true? After all, it was written 500 years after the actual thing occurred.

—Alyssa C. (age 13)

Dear Alyssa,

I am very sad to hear you can't go to church. Don't worry. Things may soon change. God can make a way for you to go to church. Keep praying and asking Him, and stay full of faith. In the meantime, you CAN be a very strong Christian, even though you can't go to church. Your salvation is all about Jesus, not people. We need the church for fellowship and spiritual growth, but God knows your situation. He is your Shepherd. He will take care of you and help you to grow.

It will be important for you to stay diligent to read your Bible regularly. You will have to be responsible to feed your spirit. Maybe you can listen to sermons on the TV or radio. Try to develop relationships with other Christians. Maybe you could get involved with a youth group or a Christian club that meets after school. You can buy some good worship CD's and spend a wonderful time enjoying the Lord in your room. Again, Christianity is about a relationship with Jesus Christ, and that relationship can grow and thrive no matter what your circumstances.

> *It is very important to know why you believe what you do.*

As far as your comment on the Bible, there is so much evidence that the Bible is historically accurate, even from non-Christian historians. The New Testament was written only 20–60 years after Jesus' death. The New Testament writers were eyewitnesses of Jesus (1 John 1:1). Many men have ventured to find a flaw in the Bible's authenticity and have ended up Christians. Some, like Josh McDowell, have written books. If you want to know more, ask for books on "apologetics" in a Christian bookstore. It is very important to know why you believe what you do. I would challenge you to allow your inquisitive mind to lead you into learning more.

If you really desire to know the Lord, you will! You can be as close to Him as you want to be! Always be a seeker.

Love, Millie

Dear Millie,

When I pray for one person specifically, I feel like I shouldn't focus only on praying for that person, and I feel guilty about not giving the same amount of prayer to other people. But when I pray for a lot of people, I kind of feel like my heart isn't into it anymore. Is it all right to pray especially hard for just one person sometimes?

— *Confused About Prayer*
(age 13)

Dear Confused About Prayer,

Absolutely! Sometimes the Holy Spirit will really keep someone on your heart so you can pray for him or her. Don't feel guilty about it. Just trust the leading of your heart in prayer. Pray for that person as often as you feel prompted. They may be going through a really difficult or dangerous time.

Many people have been awakened in the night with a strong burden to pray for someone, and later they find out that this person was in a life-threatening situation. This is the joy of being led by the Holy Spirit in prayer! If we could only peek into the spirit world and see the effects of our prayers, I'm sure we would all be praying more fervently and unceasingly.

Just trust the leading of your heart in prayer.

Keep it up, mighty prayer warrior! "Devote yourselves to prayer, being watchful and thankful," (Colossians 4:2).

Love, Millie

Dear Millie,

Sometimes I find myself thinking about really bad things that I don't want to think about. I try to get my mind off of them, but when I do, I feel really bad. What should I do? Thanks for your time.

— *Donna P. (age 11)*

Dear Donna,

First, you must know that we are all tempted with bad thoughts. Even Jesus was tempted this way by Satan. Don't feel bad about being tempted. The important thing is what you do with those thoughts.

Satan comes to plant evil thoughts in our minds. We need to know which thoughts are evil, get rid of them, and replace them with God's Word of truth. In a way, we are to be like policemen with our thoughts. 2 Corinthians 10:5 says we are to take the evil thoughts

captive and make them obey Christ. How do you know
if a thought is evil? Philippians 4:8 give us a list of
things we are to think about. If a thought enters your
mind which does not line up with Philippians 4:8, resist
the thought, and immediately replace it with God's
Word.

We are supposed to discipline
our thought life. Do not let your
thoughts wander wherever they
want. Be alert and quick to resist
anything that is against God's
truth.

We are supposed to discipline our thought life.

Secondly, make sure you are not watching, reading,
or listening to things that may cause you to have bad
thoughts. What you take in through your eyes and ears
has a strong influence on your thought life. So be careful about certain TV shows, movies, books, or music.
Spend time each day reading your Bible. Listen to
worship music before you go to bed or in the morning.
Pray often throughout the day. Focus your thoughts
and affections on Jesus throughout your day, and
there will be no room for bad thoughts to even come in.

May God grant you peace of mind.

Love, Millie

Dear Millie,

A lot of times I get really rebellious feelings toward my parents when I get in trouble. I then write bad things in my journal. Is that bad? I justify it by saying to myself, "Well, I didn't say it to their face."

—*Gwen E. (age 13)*

Dear Gwen,

It is wonderful how the Holy Spirit brings conviction of sin to our hearts. That's what He is doing in your life right now. Regardless if you write it or speak it, rebellion is a sinful condition of your heart. Your rebellious thoughts are a symptom of this. Don't let Satan cause you to excuse yourself because you don't act on it. If you allow it to go unchecked in your heart, you will eventually act it out. Like any sin, the longer it lies in the darkness, the more powerful it will become.

Now, don't get discouraged or overwhelmed. Bring the sin into the light through confession. I think it would be good to confess to your parents so they know your struggle. Tell them you don't want to rebel against them, and that you are fighting it. Ask for their prayers and support. They will gladly do that for you. If you don't feel you can be that open with your parents, then confess to someone whom you trust. If you are willing to humble yourself, admit your sin, and choose to turn from it, God will then flood you with grace and bring deliverance.

Rebellion is a sinful condition of your heart.

Stay at it. The Lord equates rebellion with witchcraft (see 1 Samuel 15:23). That's pretty sobering and shows how if not dealt with, rebellion can destroy your life and render you useless for God's work. Look at the severe consequences of Saul's disobedience. He lost the kingdom! So may you go at this with great intensity and zeal. Let every bit of it be wiped out thoroughly.

God bless you for your honesty and your passion for purity.

Love, Millie

Dear Millie,

How do you know when a book is worth reading? Several times I have picked up different books and have been amazed at the weird books there are out there! Also, how do you know the difference between a worthwhile friend and a friend who does bad things, etc.

—*Rose W. (age 10)*

Dear Rose,

Thank you for these very insightful questions. As Christians it is important that we be very discerning (which means having good judgment). We must know how to tell evil from good. Romans 12:9 says to "hate what is evil; cling to what is good." We must use discernment whenever we choose a book to read, a movie to watch, a song to listen to, or a person to befriend.

In Matthew 7:15–20, Jesus taught how to recognize evil imposters. He said to look at the fruit of their lives. A bad tree can't bear good fruit, nor can a good tree bear bad fruit. Become a fruit inspector. If you question whether someone would be good to hang out with, look at their behavior, their speech, and their attitudes. Are they rebellious, disrespectful to adults, rude, selfish, etc.? Keep in mind that nobody is perfect, but you should get a pretty good indication of the condition of their heart by these outward signs. As far as books, music, movies, etc., test their fruit by the standards and principles in God's Word. Observe carefully how you feel when you are exposed to these different forms of media. What fruit is it producing in you?

We must know how to tell evil from good.

Ask the Lord to sharpen this ability to discern. The Holy Spirit will help you discern by warning you if something is wrong by a sense of unsettledness or a lack of peace in your heart. Learn to notice these intuitions and trust your gut feelings. That's why it is so important to keep yourself in close relationship with the Lord every day. He will guard and protect you from all evil.

"Discretion will protect you, and understanding will guard you," says Proverbs 2:11.

Love, Millie

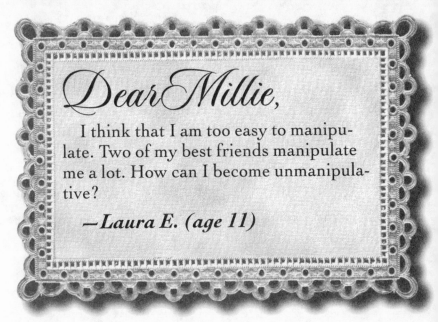

Dear Millie,

I think that I am too easy to manipulate. Two of my best friends manipulate me a lot. How can I become unmanipulative?

—*Laura E. (age 11)*

Dear Laura,

This is a very good question. Jesus has called us to be servants, but we must be led to do these acts of service by the Holy Spirit and not by people pressuring us. You are the steward of your time, your choices, and your decisions. You are responsible to God, not to other people. If He has asked you to do something, you definitely want to obey. If you are being pushed by people to do something that you don't feel God (or your parents) would want you to do, then you are putting people first in your life (this is called "men-pleasing"). This can eventually lead you to disobey

God, as in the case of Saul. Read 1 Samuel 13, where Saul gave in to the pressure of the people instead of obeying God, and see what serious consequences this had on his life!

It is very important for you to be able to say "no" to people. You must have healthy boundaries in your life. Your life is not your own — you belong to the Lord. If you let your friends control and manipulate you, then they have become your "lord". The choice is yours. Recognize that men-pleasing is a form of idolatry — having something else controlling you other than Jesus. Repent of it and ask God to remove it from your life. Your confidence and identity should stand solid in Jesus. You do not need the approval of people to feel good about yourself. Know that you are a special child of God, that the Spirit of God Almighty is living in you, and there is unlimited power and authority in His name. All this is yours. He has all you need. Don't go looking for it from people.

Your confidence and identity should stand solid in Jesus.

I pray you become bold and strong enough to make your own decisions as you hear from God. I know you will.

Love, Millie

Dear Millie,

I have no desire to be a good Christian and please God. I know this sounds funny, but I want to go to secular concerts instead of Christian concerts. Why do I feel this way and how can I change it? I am also homeschooled and I feel like I can't do anything fun. I can't even stay and listen to the sermons in my church because of what the pastor preaches on. I also can't go to all the youth group meetings every week. I feel really left out. Please help me decide what to do.

—*Nan W. (age 13)*

Dear Nan,

It sounds like you desire to get closer to Christ despite your circumstances and feelings. That is good. It's okay to be honest with God and tell Him you don't desire to be close to Him but you wish you did. Ask Him to give you a love for Him. But a more important request is to ask Him to help you understand how much He loves you. Because if you really understood how greatly He loves you, you would naturally return that love to Him. "This is love: not that we loved God, but that He loved us and sent his Son as an atoning sacrifice for our sins. . . . We love because he first loved us" (1 John 4:10, 19). So, what you need to focus on is falling in love with Jesus; getting to really know Him.

"He loved us and sent his Son."

I think if you could regularly attend your Sunday services and youth group meetings it would help you learn more about the Lord. The encouragement and fellowship with other young people would strengthen your own faith. You really need to be actively involved in your church family. It is important to speak with your parents and express to them how much you need this to keep your faith strong. Pray that God will make a way for this to happen. Also make sure you are daily reading your Bible and talking to Jesus. Remember, you need to have a relationship with Jesus. Read the Bible to hear Him speak to you and pray as you would talk with your best friend. The more you saturate yourself with godly influences—Christian books, music, friends, etc., the stronger your love and devotion for God will be.

Jesus is longing for you to have fellowship with Him. You must open the door; He will not push His way in. Set your heart to seek after Him with all your might. Oh, the treasures awaiting you there!

Love, Millie

Dear Millie,

I sometimes have doubts and fears in my relationship with God. I read my Bible every night and say my prayers too. Anyway, how can I have so much faith like you? Your books are really inspiring. But right now I'm going through a hard time and it is hard to trust in God.

—Breanna H. (age 13)

Dear Breanna,

I'm so glad you are enjoying the books and that they are inspiring you in your own Christian life. I can certainly relate to your fears and doubts. I think we all do. However, our fears and doubts can make us strong in our faith if we address them and choose to trust God.

I know it's hard to trust the Lord when things can look so bleak, but you must make the choice to do it in spite of your emotions or how things look. Keep choosing to stand on truth. God is faithful. He will never forsake you (Hebrews 13:5). If your life belongs to Him, you can trust every detail to Him. He is working His will in everything that comes your way. It is all intended for good. If you persevere and stay strong in your faith, you will find that when the trials have passed you are not the same; you have developed wings of faith that will lift you higher the next time a trial comes along. God uses each difficulty or disappointment to transform you into the image of His Beloved Son.

His love will transform you.

Keep up your devotions and seek to really understand how much God loves you. His love will transform you. You are doing well. I want to encourage you to keep it up. God loves you so much.

Love, Millie

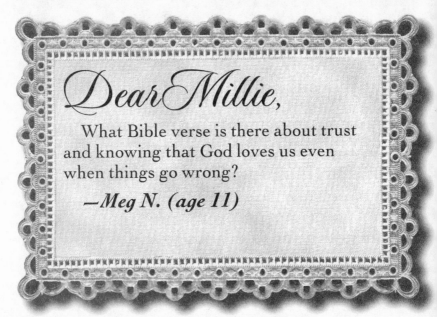

Dear Millie,

What Bible verse is there about trust and knowing that God loves us even when things go wrong?

—*Meg N. (age 11)*

Dear Meg,

It is very good to know these Scriptures, because when the storms come you need to plant your spiritual feet firmly on these promises. Romans 8:28–39 is one of my favorites; it brings me great comfort in adversity. There is nothing that can separate us from God's love and nothing bad can happen that God can't turn for good. John 16:33 is also wonderful, because they are the words of Jesus Himself. In Jesus, we can overcome all things and can have His perfect peace. The beloved Psalm 23 speaks in verse 4 of walking in dark, difficult places and yet knowing that God is with us, guiding and comforting us. He is your faithful, loving Shepherd. These are just a few; the Bible is full of many more and I challenge you to get in there and find them. Keep a section in your journal with these Scriptures written down, so when you are going through a trial, you can refer to them quickly.

Praise God for the promises in His Word, which are true and immovable! "The word of the Lord stands forever" (1 Peter 1:25).

There is nothing that can separate us from God's love.

Love, Millie

Dear Millie,

I am having trouble in my walk with God and I have found myself turning away from Him in ways like not reading my Bible, listening to gloomy music, reading, watching TV, or doing anything so I won't have to talk with Him. Please help me because I just want to cry and cry until I feel better but every time I do cry I just feel worse. I feel stressed, unhappy, and I am sorry to say, deep down inside, angry with God for hurting me.

—Katie Anne B. (age 14)

Dear Katie Anne,

It is obvious that the reason you are feeling so unhappy and stressed is because you are mad at God. It's normal to want to blame God for the bad things that happen in our lives. But is it really God's fault? Sickness, death, divorce, suffering, sorrow, etc. are the results of sin in our world. Sin is from Satan, not God.

James 1:17 says that every good and perfect thing comes from God. For an ordained time, God in His infinite wisdom has allowed sin to work its effect upon the earth. He is still in control. He works in the lives of men through faith, prayer, and the Holy Spirit. He is to be trusted always, and revered as the Almighty God, Creator of the Universe.

He has not promised us that things will go the way we want, or that we will always have it easy. Instead, He has asked us to trust Him. Isaiah 55:8 says, " 'For my thoughts are not your thoughts, neither are your ways my ways,' declares the Lord." God's ways are simply different from ours. But in all situations He is forever trustworthy.

He has asked us to trust Him.

When the bad things happen, commit them to the Lord and then look to see the good that will come from it (Romans 8:28). It may take a while to see it, but if you stay yielded and humble, He will show it to you.

Bring all of your hurts to the Lord. He will comfort you, strengthen you to endure the trial, and turn it for good in your life. Listen to Jeremiah 29:11 carefully: 'For I know the plans I have for you,' declares the Lord, 'plans to prosper you and not to harm you, plans to give you hope and a future.'

Love, Millie

Dear Millie,

Recently I was entrusted with something that did not belong to me. I was supposed to take care of it. I was scared of it and did not fulfill my duty. I got paid for the job. I lied to the owner of this thing and just yesterday confessed to them and my mom. Should I return the money? Do you think this person will keep being nice to me even though I've lost their trust?

—Andi N. (age 12)

Dear Andi,

I am very proud of you. It took courage to confess your wrongdoing. This demonstrates your desire to do what is right and to walk in the light. This is pleasing to the Lord.

I think the person who hired you would be quick to forgive since he has seen your repentant and honest heart. In fact, I believe this person will respect you for coming clean. As far as the money, I believe it is right for you to offer it back since you did not fulfill your part of the agreement. If your employer graciously gives it back, then you can keep it in good conscience.

Don't be ashamed of making mistakes. God teaches us invaluable lessons through our mistakes and failures—lessons we can learn no other way. So look back on this episode and learn from it. You are better because of it. Since you confessed and chose to walk in honesty, it was not a failure at all. It was a victory!

> *God teaches us invaluable lessons through our mistakes and failures—lessons we can learn no other way.*

Love, Millie

Dear Millie,

At church our pastor was talking about how David really lost everything he had except for God. One of his points was that we tend to fixate on the things we don't have or have lost, instead of the things we do have. It really got to me. I have realized that I am fixating on the things I don't have rather than the things I do have. I really want to be thankful, but I don't know exactly how to stop feeling sorry for myself.

—Kelsey K. (age 12)

Dear Kelsey,

It sounds like you have learned a wonderful truth in God's Word about being content and thankful. You are now in the process of trying to walk in obedience to that. I appreciate how you have taken your pastor's sermon to heart. It is never easy at first to apply God's truth to our lives. When we begin to do that, we confront the sin and selfishness that has resided in us for years. So don't expect it to be easy. There will be battles. But don't give up! You are doing right. The more you *choose* to be thankful, the more you really *will* be thankful for all the blessings in your life! Then it will come easier and you will find that God has done a work in your heart.

Thankfulness says to God, "I trust You with my life." It causes you to submit to the good *and* the bad and helps you recognize that both come from the loving hands of your Heavenly Father. Being

A thankful heart opens doors for God to bless us.

thankful means you are choosing to accept His plans for your life and that you are not insisting on your own way. A thankful heart opens doors for God to bless us, because we have learned to love Him for who He is and not just for what He gives us.

Here are some really helpful Scriptures on thankfulness which will further encourage you: 1 Thessalonians 5:18; Colossians 3:15–17; Psalm 100:4.

Thanks for encouraging us all to be more thankful every day for everything!

Love, Millie

Dear Millie,

I worry a lot about getting illnesses or diseases. I know Jesus doesn't want us to worry, and I've tried to stop, but whenever someone is sick, I get nervous. Please help!

—*Eliza D. (age 11)*

Dear Eliza,

Anxiety and worry is a horrible thing. It aims to destroy your spirit, soul, and body. It is rooted in fear. Fear is based on lies that Satan has placed in your mind that you have chosen to believe. The only way to combat fear is through God's Word.

His Word is truth; it is unchangeable, and all-powerful for destroying the lies of Satan. Take your fears and face them. You are afraid of getting sick. Do you believe God desires this for you? Of course not. Isaiah 53:5 says that by His wounds we are healed. He came to bring us life. You must choose to believe this, and when the fear of sickness comes, resist that fear and proclaim that Jesus has come to bring you life.

Are you afraid of suffering? Suppose God allows a sickness for a time. Can you trust Him in your suffering? Is your life truly God's to do with as He chooses? Deuteronomy 31:6 says, "Be strong and courageous. Do not be afraid or terrified because of them, for the Lord your God goes with you; he will never leave you nor forsake you."

The only way to combat fear is through God's Word.

2 Corinthians 1:4 promises that God will comfort us in all our afflictions. If we never experience affliction, how will we ever know the comfort of God, and therefore know how to comfort others?

I think it comes down to this: Do you really trust Him? Do you really believe He loves you and will work what is best for you in your life? If you can't wholeheartedly say "yes," then keep reading what He says in His Word and ask Him for more faith to believe. You must resist this stronghold of fear in your life. God will give you grace; you must do the warfare.

May you find total freedom from this through the blood of Jesus and the Word of truth.

Love, Millie

Dear Millie,

How can I obey my parents better and take in my punishments without putting up a fight? I've tried to act better, but when I do wrong, I feel so upset at myself and at the world. How can I get over this?

— *Becky D. (age 10)*

Dear Becky,

I'm glad you are beginning to understand how important it is to obey your parents. Ephesians 6:1–3 makes it clear how important it is to the Lord that you obey and honor your parents. Obeying and respecting your parents is the same as obeying the Lord.

Learn to receive their instruction and punishment with respect because this is what is necessary in training you and preparing you to be able to serve the Lord when you get older. If you allow rebellion to have a place in your heart, that same spirit will eventually raise itself up against the Lord sometime in your life. So, completely submit to your parents' correction and let the rebellion be driven far from you.

Romans 8:1 says, "There is now no condemnation for those who are in Christ Jesus," and 1 John 1:9 says, "If we confess our sins, he is faithful and just and will forgive us our sins and purify us from all unrighteousness."

Obeying and respecting your parents is the same as obeying the Lord.

We all sin and make mistakes. As long as you are confessing them to God and to others, if necessary, the blood of Jesus cleanses you. He is always merciful to forgive. Don't get down on yourself when you sin. Just get back up, ask God to forgive you, and ask Him to help you overcome the temptation to disobey.

In 1 John 1:9, God promises to purify us. He will eventually see to it that you are victorious over this particular sin in your life. Just be patient and receive the joy of knowing your sins are forgiven. Only Satan condemns. Jesus forgives! What a wonderful salvation we have through Jesus!

Love, Millie

Dear Millie,

I read my Bible almost every day and have a quiet time with the Lord. But when I go to school I always forget what I read. I want to remember what I read so that I can live in the Word and so other people can see the love of Jesus through me. But if I can't remember what I read, how can I "walk in the Word"?

—*Amy V. (age 13)*

Dear Amy,

I am so blessed by your sincere devotion to God's Word and your desire to make it a part of your life! Keep your daily study going. Whenever you read God's Word it transforms you, even if you don't realize it, and even if you don't think you are remembering it. God's Word is living and powerful (Hebrews 4:12). It is changing you every time you read. You don't have to make a conscious effort to remember what you read as you go through your day.

Trust the Holy Spirit to bring to your remembrance all things as you have need of them. Read John 14 for more insight on how the Holy Spirit helps us. During your day, let your heart turn toward the living Word (Jesus). John 1:14 says, "The Word became flesh and made his dwelling among us. We have seen his glory, the glory of the One and Only, who came from the Father, full of grace and truth."

Whenever you read God's Word it transforms you, even if you don't realize it.

Jesus is the total embodiment of God's Word. Let Jesus live in you each day through His Holy Spirit and you will be walking in the Word! You will become the walking Epistle you long to be.

Love, Millie

Dear Millie,

I was wondering about lying. My family has Bible time together, and in many Bible stories, Dad notes that some people lied on purpose. Men like Abraham, Moses, and others lied a few times, and God rewarded them! I have always thought that lying was bad—all the time. Do you think it is ok for me to lie or not? I think that Moses had different reasons and better judgment than me, so I shouldn't lie just because "Christians" did. What do you think?

—Lexi L. (age 13)

Dear Lexi,

I appreciate hearing from you and this is a good question. First, you must know what God says. We never base our behavior on men and their actions, but on God's Word only. The Bible states clearly that we should not lie. Colossians 3:9–10 says, "Do not lie to each other, since you have taken off your old self with its practices and have put on the new self, which is being renewed in knowledge in the image of its Creator." Leviticus 19:11 says, "Do not steal. Do not lie. Do not deceive one another."

Yes, godly men in the Bible have lied. I wouldn't go so far as to say God rewarded them for it, though. God was gracious to overlook their weakness and accomplished His plans in spite of them. You see, the Bible is full of stories of men and women who were weak and vulnerable to sin just like us. God did not put their stories in there because they lived perfect lives. He wants us to see how He can work in our lives regardless of our humanity, as long as we give ourselves completely to Him. So the Bible is full of men and women with the same sinful nature as ours. They made mistakes and sinned, but for those who followed hard after God, He used them in spite of their shortcomings. God will do the same for you. So do not get distracted by their human weaknesses and therefore justify the same sin in your life. Keep your focus on God and strive to uphold the purity of His Word. I assure you that God will do great things through you also.

> *God used them in spite of their shortcomings. God will do the same for you.*

Love, Millie

Dear Millie,

My sister was almost 5 months pregnant and then she lost the baby. I can't understand why this happened. I can't even imagine the pain she is going through. Every time I begin to think about it I just cry. I try to trust God completely, and honestly I don't know how I could get through this without Him to lean on. I know that He never leaves us or forsakes us, but at the same time I just can't understand why this happened. How do I deal with this?
—*Lisa M. (age 16)*

Dear Lisa,

My heart goes out to you and your family in this loss. I understand the anger, shock, and broken hearts and shattered dreams. Don't be afraid to experience all of these different emotions, as it is part of the grieving process. The more you are able to get it out, the quicker you will move toward healing. It may seem like you and your family will never recover, but you will. And if you do not let bitterness settle in your heart, you will not only recover, but you will also be stronger because of it.

Since the Fall in the Garden of Eden, sin has worked its effect into our lives, causing suffering, pain, sickness, and death. Christians are not exempt from these things, but we do have the promise of Jesus' presence to comfort and strengthen us. We also have the ability to look at tragedy and know that God can use it for good. Romans 8:28 says, "And we know that in all things God works for the GOOD of those who love him, who have been called according to his purpose." It may be hard to believe that a baby dying could bring about any good. But never forget that our God is a Mighty Redeemer.

> *Never forget that our God is a Mighty Redeemer.*

May God sustain you with His peace, and may your faith remain unwavering. May you proclaim with the countless saints who are suffering around the world, "God is good all the time!" When you can do this, you will rise up with renewed strength, and God will use you to strengthen those around you in their suffering.

My condolences to you and your family.

Love, Millie

Dear Millie,

My boyfriend and I are both Christians, except we live 3 hours apart (I met him at camp). Do you have any ideas to help keep us going, like studying Bible passages or anything? I know that our relationship will hit some hard times with us living apart, but we do plan on visiting.

—*Wendy B. (age 14)*

Dear Wendy,

Let me encourage you first, as with all things, to surrender this relationship to God. Ask Him if it would honor and please Him for you to continue this relationship. If God is blessing it, you will not need to be concerned about keeping it going. Any relationship where God is at the center will not require a lot of striving on our part to keep it strong.

You are a bit young to get really serious with a boy, so try to keep it from consuming your attention. Let this friendship take shape naturally and don't try to force anything. That's the joy of keeping things surrendered to the Lord. You can rest in the situation and enjoy it for what it is and release God to have His way in it.

Since you are both Christians, do all you can to keep Jesus in the center of your friendship. When you talk, share what God is doing in your life, exchange Scriptures, and pray for each other.

Let this friendship take shape naturally.

Try to keep the right perspective on your relationship. Look at him as a brother in Christ. Keep your focus on serving the Lord and trust Him to work His will out in your life. "In all your ways acknowledge him [put Him first and commit to Him everything], and he will make your paths straight" (Proverbs 3:6).

Love, Millie

Dear Millie,

My mom told me that if you give out your affections too easily (to boys), when you get married you don't have anything for your husband. Does that include thinking that boys are cute? Please give me your insight.

— *Lydia D. (age 12)*

Dear Lydia,

Your mom is telling you to guard your heart and save your affections for the man who will one day become your husband. This is very true. You don't want to pour your emotions and affections into a relationship that will not be a lifetime commitment.

Does it mean you won't be attracted to boys? No, of course not. It is only normal for you to be interested in or have an attraction toward boys. You can enjoy their friendship as brothers in the Lord, keeping romance out of it. I know this sounds hard to do, but you will know when you have allowed your heart to get too involved. Then you will have to pull back and rein in those emotions.

I hope this is helpful. There are many good resources in Christian bookstores on dating. These may help give you more understanding.

Love, Millie

> *You don't want to pour your emotions and affections into a relationship that will not be a lifetime commitment.*

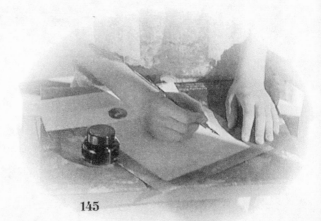

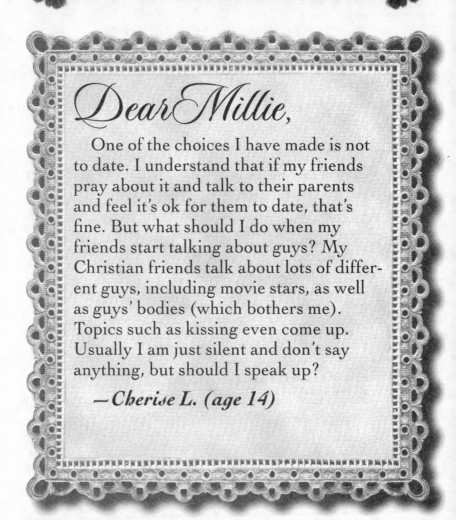

Dear Millie,

One of the choices I have made is not to date. I understand that if my friends pray about it and talk to their parents and feel it's ok for them to date, that's fine. But what should I do when my friends start talking about guys? My Christian friends talk about lots of different guys, including movie stars, as well as guys' bodies (which bothers me). Topics such as kissing even come up. Usually I am just silent and don't say anything, but should I speak up?

—*Cherise L. (age 14)*

Dear Cherise,

That's a good question, and a tough situation to be in. I know you don't want your friends to think you're so spiritual that they can't relate to you. You'll have to determine where to draw the lines.

I believe the Holy Spirit will make you feel uncomfortable to listen to really inappropriate conversations. In this case you can discreetly slip out of the room or try changing the subject. They may ask why you won't join them, and then you can freely express your opinions. It's okay to speak up if you feel the conversation is really going the wrong direction. That's part of being a leader. You may need to guide your friends back to more wholesome discussions. Ask the Lord to give you wisdom. Much of it will depend on how close you are to the girls and how much they can receive from you.

You may need to guide your friends back to more wholesome discussions.

I appreciate your convictions and your desire to remain pure in thought, speech, and behavior. This brings such glory to God! May you find boldness to speak up when you should and wisdom to know when to remain silent.

"Don't let anyone look down on you because you are young, but set an example for the believers in speech, in life, in love, in faith and in purity" (1 Timothy 4:12).

Love, Millie

Dear Millie,

I do not believe that I will want a husband and children when I am older. Am I right to think this way? My friend told me that I was being silly about this, and now I'm confused. Thank you for helping me as well as all the others who have written to you.

—*Micah D. (age 15)*

Dear Micah,

Thanks for sharing your thoughts and concerns with me. I understand that at this age you cannot even imagine a husband and children, nor even desire it. When I was your age, I too planned to live a life of singleness like my Aunt Wealthy. Don't feel bad about that. You are only being honest with where you are now. But at the same time stay open to this possibility for your future.

If you have made Jesus your Lord, then He holds your future in His hands. If He has planned for you to have a husband and children when you are grown, then your heart will delight in this and it will be an incredible joy and blessing. You do not need to concern yourself with it now; just keep your heart open to this being a possibility as you submit yourself to God's plan for your life.

One of my favorite verses, Proverbs 3:5–6, says; "Trust in the Lord with all your heart and lean not on your own understanding; in all your ways acknowledge him, and he will make your paths straight."

He holds your future in His hands.

Trust Him to direct your path and rest in knowing it will be good!

Love, Millie

Dear Millie,

I have a boyfriend and we are frequently alone. We go to the movies, bake cookies together, or play board games. We never do anything bad. Yes, we hold hands, but who says that is bad? In my church, holding hands is a good thing. We do it at the "Our Father" and at "peace time." What's so bad about having a boyfriend if we are both responsible? Is it just not good at my age?

—*Alexandra T. (age 15)*

Dear Alexandra,

Thanks for your question. It will be helpful to others. This issue of dating is something each family will have to consider carefully. You must spend plenty of time asking the Lord and talking with your parents and spiritual leaders. You are old enough to receive counsel and guidance from the Lord and others so you can make responsible decisions. Here are some principles to keep in mind when considering this area of dating:

First, your body is the temple of the Holy Spirit (1 Corinthians 6:19). You are commanded to keep it pure and holy—spiritually, emotionally, and physically. You must avoid placing yourself in a position where you will be tempted to fall into any sexual sin. Holding hands and being alone together can lead to possible temptation. *Be careful not to think you are stronger than you really are.*

Also, you must protect yourself emotionally. If you become too emotionally entangled with someone now, when the relationship ends it will cause a lot of hurt and disillusionment. You are at a wonderful time in your life when you should enjoy a variety of relationships instead of tying yourself down to one person. Limiting yourself to one boy too early could thwart the process of blossoming into the fullness of who you are called to be.

The most important relationship you must nurture is your relationship with the Lord. A romantic relationship can actually distract you from pursuing the Lord and serving Him. I would hate for you to miss the beauty and freedom of these youthful years during which you could spend time developing your walk with the Lord, participating in church outreaches, and getting involved in other youth functions.

After carefully considering the above, praying, and receiving godly counsel, I'm sure you will make the most righteous decision for your life right now.

Love, Millie

Dear Millie,

I have a problem. I have romantic feelings for a boy. I don't like feeling this way because I firmly believe in courtship and I'm way too young to know what I'm feeling. I've tried to stop liking him in that way and I am trying to think of him as just a friend, since he is 17 and I'm just 13, but I can't seem to do it! I've been praying really hard about this and have asked to see God's will, but how can I banish these feelings? I WANT to do it, but it just isn't working!

—Shelly L. (age 13)

Dear Shelly,

You are doing so well! You are fighting the fight of faith. Don't get frustrated! Your emotions will eventually line up with your convictions. Just stay strong in your spirit, take control of your thoughts, and stay focused on your relationship with God. Try to avoid dwelling on those romantic feelings and emotions, but rather, keep your heart and affections on Him.

Sometimes it takes a while for breakthroughs to come. God will honor your heart to stay pure and undistracted. You will experience these romantic feelings often. It is not a sin to feel this way, nor is it necessarily wrong or abnormal. What you are doing is establishing standards for your life. You are choosing to keep your affections under the Lordship of Christ. *You* are in control, not your emotions. Even though your emotions may still flare up, it doesn't mean you have to give in to them. So don't let them consume you. Just keep your focus on the Lord. As you seek God with all your heart, mind, and will, your emotions will follow.

> *God will honor your heart to stay pure and undistracted.*

I commend you for your maturity and passion for purity. You will have a great impact on your generation.

"Flee the evil desires of youth, and pursue righteousness, faith, love and peace, along with those who call on the Lord out of a pure heart" (2 Timothy 2:22).

Love, Millie

Dear Millie,

I have a friend who likes me for more than a friend and I'm afraid I like him too, but I don't think he's really given his heart to God. He talks about magic and says he has "powers" but he says he believes in God. I thought that magic was of the devil. I don't understand what God needs me to do, because I know that somehow I'm supposed to reach out to my friend and I don't know how. Please give me some guidance.

—Almost Helpless (age 13)

Dear Almost Helpless,

Thanks for writing. I am a bit concerned for you and this relationship. Your friend may believe in God and still not be saved. James 2:19 tells us that even the demons believe in God. It sounds like he could be dabbling in witchcraft, because that's what magical powers are. This is more dangerous than you could imagine.

God has power, but this comes through the Holy Spirit, not magic. I would recommend that you very honestly tell him of your concerns about this.

I would also encourage you to pull back from him so you can get your emotions in check.

2 Corinthians 6:14–18 warns against having any form of a binding relationship with unbelievers. I believe this includes dating or any kind of emotional attachments where you allow vulnerable intimacy of your soul. Do not put yourself into a situation where you will be tempted to compromise your faith. This friend could easily influence you away from your love and devotion to the Lord.

The safest thing is to pray for him and speak boldly of your faith.

The safest thing is to pray for him and speak boldly of your faith. Let him know exactly where you stand as far as your friendship with him and where you draw the lines. You could also invite him to church, youth group functions, or other Christian social activities.

Keep your heart pure and set on the Lord. Beware of subtle traps that could hinder you from running the race of faith. Read Hebrews 12:1 and cling to it.

I believe God will give you wisdom and grace in dealing with your friend if you set your heart to honor Him above all else.

Love, Millie

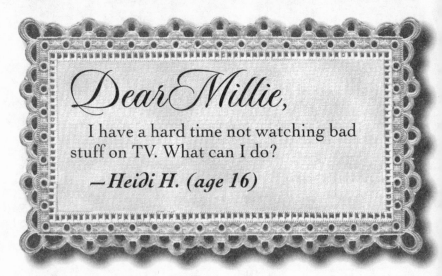

Dear Millie,

I have a hard time not watching bad
stuff on TV. What can I do?

—Heidi H. (age 16)

Dear Heidi,

I'm so glad that you are concerned with this problem. Watching TV can actually become an addiction. It is better to break these addictions while you are young, so this is the best time to start.

First, ask God for a real sensitivity and conviction to turn away from the pollution and evil that is rampant in today's television programming. Remember your body is a temple for the Holy Spirit. If you want the presence of God with you, then you must set an environment of holiness in your heart and mind. What you allow to come in through your eyes and ears will lodge in your soul. It happens very subtly and slowly. Unrighteous attitudes, lust, and unclean thoughts begin to take root and grow in your heart if you are not careful to guard what enters your soul. Write out Psalm 101:2–3 and put it on your bathroom mirror. Let it be your desire and the cry of your heart.

Allow yourself one show a night or a few shows a week that are safe and wholesome. Try to set limits. If you are unable to control what you watch, then do not allow yourself to watch any TV. Stick with renting wholesome movies. You should also confess your struggle with your parents and let them help you set boundaries and hold you accountable.

> *Set an environment of holiness in your heart and mind.*

Pursue your devotional time and get plenty of fellowship at church. This is a spiritual battle, so fight it with prayer and the Word of God. Once you overcome, you will have more authority and faith to combat other temptations that come your way. As believers we must have self-control. We must be able to say "no" to evil in any form and not allow our flesh to have its way. This will be a battle you will fight your whole life, so learn to be a warrior now while you are young.

I pray that God will give you complete victory to slay this giant in your life. Don't quit until you have the complete victory!

Love, Millie

Dear Millie,

I have a really hard time controlling my thoughts. Lately, I have seen some things or read things (completely by accident) and I can't get them out of my head. It's scary how messed up the world is — sometimes I just cannot get away from inappropriate things on TV or the Internet (especially the Internet!). I hate feeling this way; I feel impure, though I have asked God to forgive me for seeing these things, even if I didn't mean to, and clear my mind of them. They bombard all my prayers and it's starting to scare me. How do I "master my thoughts"?

—*Feeling Bad (age 13)*

Dear Feeling Bad,

Staying pure in the midst of a defiled world is one of our biggest battles as Christians. Fighting this battle is especially hard for young people. Satan has set so many traps out there. You are absolutely right in realizing that the battle begins with your thoughts. You must learn how to master your thoughts. Romans 8:5 tells us that those who live in accordance with the Spirit have their minds set on what the Spirit desires. How do we live in accordance with the Spirit? By the power of the Holy Spirit and God's Word of truth (John 17:17).

Our mind, spirit, and soul are washed and cleansed when we set our minds on the truth of God's Word and lean fully on the power of the Holy Spirit to purify us. As you begin taking action to combat these unclean thoughts, I recom-

Discipline your thoughts to turn to God's Word.

mend that you memorize a passage of Scripture and begin to recite it when you feel bombarded with disturbing thoughts or images. Discipline your thoughts to turn to God's Word, especially when the temptations come. I also suggest studying Romans chapters 6, 7, and 8, as they address this struggle.

You could also choose one of the Psalms to memorize. Meditate on God's wonderful attributes (His character and personality). Let your thoughts be absorbed with Him and continually trust in the Holy Spirit to wash and cleanse you each day. It does take effort to begin this new way of thinking, but the Holy Spirit will encourage you, and soon you will rise above this struggle!

May you find renewed strength to fight this battle and be completely restored in your thought life.

Love, Millie

Dear Millie,

My mom says that girls' bodies begin to change when they're around my age. Girls my age are starting to develop, but I haven't even started changing. I want to be mature like the other girls. So my first question is: How can I look at this in a godly way? Also, I know that I am too young to date. I don't know if it's wrong for me to think boys are cute. It's hard for me not to want to kiss the cute ones.
—*Little Kid C. (age 11)*

Dear Little Kid,

I'm glad you and your mom have had discussions about the changes your body will soon be going through. I will be glad to answer your questions, as I know you can freely discuss things with your mom also. Don't ever hesitate to ask her anything on your mind. Sometimes you can be misled by things you read or things you hear from other girls.

My encouragement to you is to trust God. Your body was uniquely designed by God and is not like anybody

else's. Everybody goes through physical changes at different times. You cannot compare your body to others. Some girls change early, and others later. It is not important where you are on the timing. It will happen in God's perfect time for you, so try not to worry about it and trust the Lord.

Everybody goes through physical changes at different times.

It is very normal for you to be attracted to boys. This too is part of the way you are changing and growing into a woman. However, you should not allow it to control your thoughts and emotions. For instance, you do not want to be thinking about kissing boys. This is not appropriate behavior and therefore you need to cut off the thoughts that may tempt or distract you. Stay in control of your emotions. Try to avoid excessive emotional attachments or crushes.

It is important to establish your convictions about boys and dating now. This is something that needs to be worked out with your parents. Set guidelines with your parents that you can keep through your teen years. These convictions and standards will serve as a map, compass, and shield to keep you out of dangerous waters. You can't start a journey without them, so that's why you must think about it now while you are just beginning.

Thanks for writing about these personal issues. You won't be signing your name "Little Kid" much longer.

Love, Millie

Dear Millie,

I am confused about clothes! What do you think is modest enough without looking ridiculous?
—*Ashley A. (age 11)*

Dear Ashley,

I am so pleased you asked such a question. It shows a depth of maturity and sincerity in pleasing the Lord.

1 Timothy 2:9 instructs women to dress modestly, with decency and propriety. How you define what "modesty" is will be up to you and your parents. Here are some further guidelines to consider: Beware of drawing inappropriate attention to yourself. Watch low necklines, excessively tight pants and tops, and very short skirts and shorts. If you're not sure, ask your parents what they think. Also, listen closely to your conscience. That is how the Holy Spirit speaks to you.

You are at the right age to consider these things and lay a godly foundation. We do not want to dishonor the

Lord in any way. Our bodies are His temple and we must be very careful to glorify God in all we do. How we dress speaks loudly to others. We give off signals by our appearance. If we dress immodestly, others take us as being loose and immoral. Our outward appearance gives an indication of what is in our hearts.

Thank you for your question and your passion for purity in all things. I hope this will encourage other girls to carefully consider what kind of impression they are giving off by how they dress.

Our outward appearance gives an indication of what is in our hearts.

Love, Millie

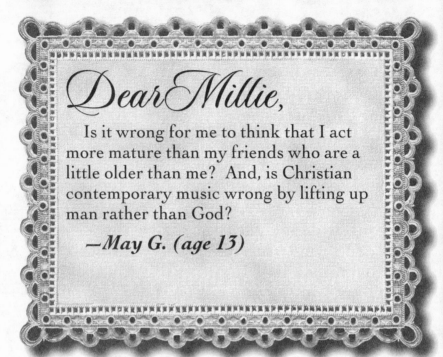

Dear Millie,

Is it wrong for me to think that I act more mature than my friends who are a little older than me? And, is Christian contemporary music wrong by lifting up man rather than God?

—*May G. (age 13)*

Dear May,

I do not think it is wrong to have honest evaluations about yourself. You may be more mature because of your faith, your background, or other reasons. It is fine to be aware of that, but beware of the trap of believing that you are superior to others. If you are graced with maturity beyond your years, there comes with this grace a responsibility of being a godly leader.

Jesus said the greatest of all is a servant (Matthew 20:26). Leaders are servants. It is sobering and humbling to be in that position. Don't shrink from it out of fear of the responsibility, but accept it as a calling of God and lean on Him to show you how to lead righteously.

In regards to Christian music (or other forms of media in which people are put into the spotlight), there is always the temptation to exalt men. This happens because we are part of a fallen world. But we should look for the truth and righteousness in the music, because there is a lot of good in contemporary Christian music.

Jesus said the greatest of all is a servant.

The important thing for you to be concerned about is your own heart. If you feel the music is a stumbling block for you and causes you to idolize men, then maybe you should avoid the live concerts and just casually listen to it on the radio. Make your own boundaries. Ask yourself: Is this controlling me, or am I able to control it? Has it become so important to me that I can't do without it? What are the effects on my spiritual life? This type of evaluation is an important part of maturing and growing in the Lord. What is acceptable for others may not be acceptable for you.

May you grow in the grace and goodness of our Lord Jesus.

Love, Millie

Dear Millie,

I have a terrible problem with being very snoopy. I'm always going through my older brother's stuff. I read his letters from other girls and look through his private journals. I can't stop and if I am stupid enough to tell him what I was doing, I'd hate to think what he'd do! Today he almost caught me. I acted like I was getting a book. I don't want to stop, but I'm so afraid I'll get caught.

—*Snoop (age 14)*

Dear Snoop,

Thanks for your confession. It sounds like you are not convinced enough that what you are doing is wrong. Allow me to convince you. Snooping and then lying about it is very deceptive. Snooping is invading other people's privacy. It is an ungodly curiosity that could easily lead to other similar problems, such as gossiping and being a busybody and other things that are worse. 1 Timothy 5:13 warns against being idlers, gossips, and busybodies. This is not pleasing behavior to the Lord.

In Matthew 7:12, Jesus said to treat others as you would have them treat you. Would you want others poking around in your journals and diaries? There is a biblical principle called the law of reaping and sowing (see Galatians 6:7). If you continue to sow this sinful behavior, you will find yourself reaping an equally unpleasant intrusion yourself someday.

> *It is an ungodly curiosity.*

Hopefully, God's Word has convicted you and knowing that this displeases the Lord will be a great motivation to stop. Put snooping behind you and use your time to do something to serve or bless your brother instead. God wants the very best for you, and so do I.

Love, Millie

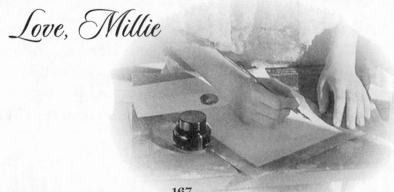

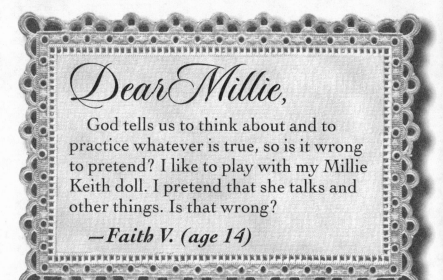

Dear Millie,

God tells us to think about and to practice whatever is true, so is it wrong to pretend? I like to play with my Millie Keith doll. I pretend that she talks and other things. Is that wrong?

—*Faith V. (age 14)*

Dear Faith,

What a great question! It shows your heart is very concerned with pleasing the Lord. I am encouraged by your sensitivity and desire to live a life of faith that honors God.

Let me assure you that it is perfectly fine to pretend with your dolls. The Scripture you referred to is found in Philippians 4:8, and it is a wonderful verse that helps us with our thoughts. When you play with your dolls, you are not being deceived nor practicing deceit. This is the big difference.

Deception is being misled to believe what is false, or leading others to believe what is false. Philippians 4:8 teaches us the opposite. It teaches us to think about truth and things that are excellent and praiseworthy. Pretending with your dolls is very innocent and healthy. You are developing your creativity

Pretending with your dolls is very innocent and healthy.

and establishing your values. God created children to have this wonderful ability to prepare them for the responsibilities in adulthood. So relax, enjoy your dolls, and include Jesus in the fun!

Love, Millie

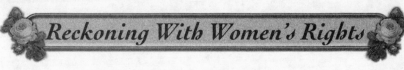

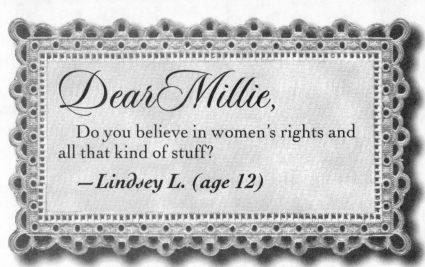

Dear Millie,

Do you believe in women's rights and all that kind of stuff?

— *Lindsey L. (age 12)*

Dear Lindsey,

The Bible tells us that in the Kingdom of God, "There is neither Jew nor Greek, slave nor free, male nor female, for you are all one in Christ Jesus" (Galatians 3:28). We are all equal in Christ; we just have different roles. Jesus was the great liberator of women. I love to read the stories of how Jesus related to women. He readily spoke with them when others would not (the Samaritan woman at the well). He stood against the injustices of the law against women during that time (the woman caught in adultery). He was born of a woman, and women were there at His death (Mary Magdalene, Mary the mother of James and John, and Salome). Women were there to serve

Him during His ministry and after His death. After His resurrection, He first appeared to a woman (Mary Magdalene).

Jesus demonstrated that women were equally honored among His followers. I, therefore, do not believe there should be any form of discrimination against women. However, we must be careful that we don't go around demanding our rights. This would not be the attitude of Jesus either, who also set the example of how to suffer under injustices (1 Peter 2:21–23). It's the inner quality of a gentle and quiet spirit that pleases God (1 Peter 3:4). I believe it's sad that women have resorted to pushy and aggressive behavior to obtain their rights, and in the process, have lost what is most precious.

Jesus was the great liberator of women.

May God form in you that beautiful balance of a godly woman — confident in your value as a person and walking in a spirit of gentleness.

Love, Millie

Dear Millie,

I HATE my piano teacher! He stinks, wears big chunky glasses, and doesn't clip his nails. I end up being really rude. My parents won't let me get another teacher. Am I the only girl in the world with a problem like this? PLEASE help!

—*Rude Student (age 11)*

Dear Rude,

Well, your situation is quite unique, but the problem you are struggling with is common to us all: loving the unlovable. We all know people who are unpleasant to be around, whatever the reason. God has placed them there to teach us something very important. He wants us to learn to love, to look beyond the outward appearance, and see them as God sees them. I learned this important lesson when I met Damaris Drybread. It was very hard to like her, but God taught me so much as I turned to Him for help.

Loving an Unpleasant Person

When you begin to see people the way God sees them, the first thing that happens, as you have found, is that you see your true heart. You see how unable you are to love and how irritated and unkind you feel. But God is able to love him through you. He can give you mercy and compassion for this man. When you receive God's love into your life, you can begin to get past your self-centeredness and become more concerned about others. Keep asking God for this. Regardless of his appearance, this man deserves your respect and courtesy as your teacher.

> *Regardless of his appearance, this man deserves your respect and courtesy as your teacher.*

Submit to your parents' decision about keeping your piano teacher. Give God time to work in your heart and give him a chance. If after a while you still feel you want to change teachers, talk to your parents about it again. But before you seek to get out of this difficulty, make sure you have learned what God wants to teach you.

Thanks for writing.

Love, Millie

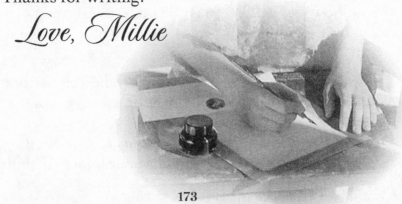

Dear Millie,

Every Sunday we go to a local nursing home. I HATE the nursing home! It smells, the people smell, and I hate it. My mom said I should develop a love for these people but it's hard to show love to people who dribble! I know this sounds mean but I want help!

—Unloving N. (age 11)

Dear Unloving,

Well, you gave me a good chuckle and I certainly find your honesty refreshing. It is okay to be honest about how we feel. We must be honest with the Lord also. It doesn't mean it's right, but it is okay to face the truth.

Now, let's face the truth together. You recognize that you have a lack of love for these poor, pitiful people in the nursing home. Right now you can't get past your senses—what you see, smell, etc. You are stuck in the natural world and you are stuck in your human inability to love. I understand this. You must ask God to get you past your "self." Ask Him to help you see past the dribbling, the smell of urine, and the stained furniture. Ask Him to let you see the painful, lonely, suffering needs in their hearts. Ask Him to let you feel His love and compassion for these people, who are His children. They have been forsaken, despised, and often mistreated. They are the helpless outcasts of our society. What do you think God's heart is for them?

When Jesus came, whom did He hang out with? Did He avoid the demon-possessed child who drooled and convulsed wickedly? Did He despise the crippled, the lepers, the poor, and the needy? Never! He touched them, wept with them, and healed them. Allow yourself to see the need and feel the pain and you will quickly go beyond yourself. Your mother is wise to take you there and expose you to those who are suffering, otherwise you will never know how most of the world lives. It is so easy at your age to feel like the world revolves around you and that everyone lives like you do. So *allow yourself to be stretched* and ask God to help you begin to find at least one person to show some love and kindness to. It doesn't take much—a smile, a drink of water, a prayer. You have so much to offer them. As you step out in boldness and choose to be the hands and feet of Jesus, you will feel more satisfaction and blessing than anything else could give you!

Thanks for writing.

Love, Millie

Dear Millie,

I have my own laptop and I LOVE being on the Internet. But I lie a lot to people when I'm online. I used to think it's no big deal and not sinful because I don't know the people I'm chatting with. But now I'm tangled in a web of lies that even affects the people I know, and they will never trust me again. Please help with my lying.

— **Jenny C. (age 13)**

Dear Jenny,

God is working in your heart! The Holy Spirit is gently convicting you of your sins and drawing you toward repentance! This is good news!

First, I strongly urge you to confess your sins to your parents. Tell them about the lying on the Internet, and that God is stirring this conviction in your heart.

Next, come clean with your friends. Confess the truth. You do risk losing the trust of some friends, but that is the consequence that stems from lying. Don't fear how others will respond. Your main concern now is getting right with God, with your parents, and with your friends. These are hard steps to take, but God will honor you for your repentance. You can grow in maturity by being obedient to God. These are hard lessons to learn, but they are valuable lessons. So don't be afraid— walk in courage and seek the help of your parents.

It is my personal opinion that it is very dangerous to chat with strangers online. However, if you parents permit this, DO NOT give out your real name or any information about where you live or go to school. Many people use a "screen name" online to protect their identity and privacy. This is very appropriate and very important for a girl your age. Ask your parents to help you set healthy boundaries with the people you meet online, and do not cross those boundaries.

If you submit your Internet usage to God and your parents you will enjoy a renewed relationship with God from a clean conscience.

Love, Millie

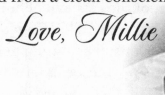

Dear Millie,

My cousin is really getting into witch-craft and books about that stuff. When we were little, before I came to know God, we would pretend to be witches. But I have asked forgiveness from God. I have prayed for my cousin, but I want to know how to help her. Please help.

— *Worried About Cousin (age 11)*

Dear Worried,

Your concern for your cousin is well-founded. Witchcraft is never anything to play with or to treat lightly. Your cousin is ignorant of the real evil behind it. By all means, keep praying for her and keep encouraging her to avoid such things. Consider inviting her to church activities, Bible studies, etc., but be careful not to lecture her or scold her. She will feel you are being self-righteous. Rather, plead with her and tell her you are genuinely concerned for her well-being. Tell her those things are real and can be very dangerous to her soul and spirit. If she gets angry or defensive, you will just have to let it drop and keep praying for her salvation.

There is great power in your prayers for her. Remember, "The one who is in you is greater than the one who is in the world" (1 John 4:4). You can pray that she will totally lose interest in such things and shut those demonic doors into her spirit. She is blessed to have such a caring cousin. God will reach her. Keep on loving her and be a faithful friend.

> *Witchcraft is never anything to play with or to treat lightly.*

Love, Millie

Dear Millie,

Some people say we should not read stories about witchcraft. Why not? If we don't believe in it, why can't we just enjoy the books? It is only fiction. Besides, if we were to give up all books with witchcraft in them we would have to give up some of the great classics. Just because we read these books doesn't mean we are bad people. Many people have put their views on life in books, whether in between the lines or straight out. Why should we be deprived of seeing the world in all different perspectives? I believe in and love God very much. Is there anything wrong with my thinking?

—Holly B. (age 14)

Dear Holly,

First, I want to encourage you in your desire to know truth. We must always look carefully at why we believe a certain way.

Literature and Witchcraft

Let me start by saying that witchcraft and Satan are very real. The powers of wickedness in the spiritual realm are as real as the power of God and His angels. This is taught throughout the Bible, and witchcraft was strongly warned against in the Old Testament (Exodus 22:18). Be wise and aware that witchcraft is not some fantasy or fable! Here are some principles to consider as you seek out what's right for you:

First, consult God's Word. Proverbs 3:7 says, "Do not be wise in your own eyes; fear the Lord and *shun* evil." Sometimes the Bible does not directly address a certain issue. You must then look at God's principles and truths to find an answer, such as Philippians 4:8. Use this Scripture as a standard for what you read, what you listen to, and what you watch.

Second, always submit to those in authority: namely, your parents. Get their counsel. Ask them to pray about it with you. Third, test the fruit. How does the book affect your soul? Does it give you nightmares? Does it affect your devotion to the Lord? Only you can honestly evaluate this.

Last, but most important, sincerely pray and ask God how He feels about it. Let the Holy Spirit guide you and help you discern what is good for you and what is not.

The responsibility of the choice is yours. If you prayerfully consider and explore the above principles and still feel liberty to read the books, then the opinions of others may not matter. What is okay for one may not be for another.

Love, Millie

Collect all of our Millie products!

A Life of Faith: Millie Keith Series

Collect our other
A Life of Faith Products!

A Life of Faith: Elsie Dinsmore

Check out
www.alifeoffaith.com

🌹 Get news about Millie and her cousin Elsie

🌹 Find out more about the 19th century world they live in

🌹 Learn to live a life of faith like they do

🌹 Learn how they overcome the difficulties we all face in life

🌹 Find out about Millie and Elsie products

🌹 Join our girls' club

A Life of Faith Books
"It's Like Having a Best Friend From Another Time"

Do you want to live a life of faith?
Are you interested in having a stronger devotional life?
Millie's Daily Diary can help you!

MILLIE'S DAILY DIARY
A Personal Journal for Girls

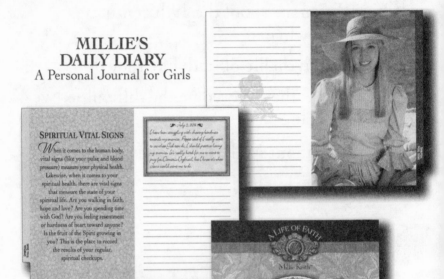

SPIRITUAL VITAL SIGNS

When it comes to the human body, vital signs (like your pulse and blood pressure) measure your physical health. Likewise, when it comes to your spiritual health, there are vital signs that measure the state of your spiritual life. Are you walking in faith, hope and love? Are you spending time with God? Are you feeling resentment or hardness of heart toward anyone? Is the fruit of the Spirit growing in you? This is the place to record the results of your regular, spiritual checkups.

Full of beautiful color photos of Millie, this journal has the unique feature of tabbed sections so that entries can be made in different categories — daily reflections, prayers, answers to prayer, favorite Scriptures, goals & dreams, and more.

Available at your local bookstore